LADY Serena's CHOICE

Lady Serena's Choice

JEWEL ALLEN

Mirror Press

Interior Design by Cora Johnson

Edited by Donna Hatch, Joanne Lui, and Lorie Humpherys

Cover design by Josephine Blake and Rachael Anderson; Image compositing by Caralyn Young

Published by Mirror Press, LLC

Timeless Romance Anthology® is a registered trademark of Mirror Press, LLC

ISBN: 978-1-952611-06-3

Lady Serena's Choice

Lady Serena would rather ride horses than dance in the ballroom. And no one matches her passion for horses and makes her feel more alive than her father's groom, Sebastian Bromley. As the daughter of a duke, however, she knows she may never act on her feelings or risk a scandal.

Sebastian Bromley has a job that many in the working class would envy—as groom in the Duke of Delaval's horse stables. But Sebastian aspires to go to America where he can create a name and wealth for himself using his horse acumen. Until then, he must hide his love for Lady Serena, the beautiful daughter of the house.

Even as Lady Serena and Sebastian fulfill their duties, a winter stranding pushes their mutual feelings to the surface. When their hearts yearn for what society forbids, choosing love means risking it all.

One

Leitham Park, Derryshire

In the summer, Lady Serena Clarke turned brown as a wild truffle. This was owing to the fact that she spent a lot of time outdoors on her beloved horse, Crumpet.

The governess chastised her charge more than once that as the oldest daughter of the Duke of Delaval, she wasn't acting in ways befitting her station, but Serena simply laughed it off.

"My future husband must tolerate the smell of horses, for that is my favorite perfume," she would say cheekily. The knowledge that a duke's daughter could get away more easily with eccentricities emboldened her.

Crumpet, officially known as Her Lady Biscuit, turned a pretty dappled gray in the summer months. She had a high step and sweet manners, although she liked to run off with her rider rather uncontained through the grounds of the Delaval estate—which suited Serena just fine.

"It takes nerves of steel to gallop that fast," Serena often mused out loud, though when questioned further, she denied unequivocally that she knew this from firsthand experience.

The Delaval estate sprawled on thousands of acres atop a hill by the sea in Derryshire. Serena often rode the grounds to the cliffs overlooking the swirling waters. With the wind buffeting her and Crumpet, she often imagined herself the heroine in battles that had taken place on those very shores.

The year Serena's mother fell ill with a mysterious malady that kept her bedridden, the duke hired a new head groom. Jonathan Bromley brought with him his sixteen-year-old son, Sebastian, who was two years older than Serena.

Serena knew everyone by name at the stables. She didn't put on airs as the duke's firstborn daughter. Though she expected to be treated with respect, she wanted to be friendly and informal with the staff. Her interest was simply in the welfare of the animals, not worrying about being proper.

The duke's horses numbered nearly thirty, all of impeccable breeding. The Duke of Delaval had made a name for himself among horse circles that he could conjure up a horse with the perfect characteristics as requested by a buyer.

Crumpet herself was descended from the Godolphin Arabian legend Sumira, and good English stock, the combination of which produced a fine thoroughbred sought out by the most particular of horse breeders.

When the new head groom and his son crossed paths with Serena, she went out of her way to make them feel at home. Horses were their common ground, and soon, Serena and the elder Bromley were engaged in animated conversations about horses he'd worked with in his storied career at many grand houses.

Serena came alive during these discourses. She could simply sit for hours listening to Jonathan spout off anecdote after anecdote, while his son Sebastian said hardly anything.

She would turn to Jonathan and ask if Sebastian knew how to speak, which rendered the young man rosy-cheeked with embarrassment.

Soon, it became a game for fourteen-year-old Serena—to get Sebastian Bromley to speak more than two words in her presence.

"Sebastian, does Crumpet need new shoes?"

Without speaking, Sebastian would lift Crumpet's hooves and shake his head or nod.

"Sebastian, what did you think of my run this morning?"

Sebastian would smile and nod with approval.

"Sebastian, why won't you talk to me?"

He would point at himself with a question in his gaze.

Leading Serena to roll her eyes and huff out of the stables.

As head groom, Jonathan was charged with teaching Serena and her two younger sisters how to ride. Her older brother, Quinn, had no interest in horses unless he was mounted for a fox hunt. Serena considered herself beyond teaching; she bristled at the thought of someone molding her natural horsemanship into a rigid technique. If she were to be quizzed about riding, she would have no ability to voice what she was doing. She could demonstrate the method, however.

Serena thought Jonathan a smart man; he didn't try to curb her enthusiasm for the saddle. He did come along on her rides, so she could explore farther out from the main house. They often brought Sebastian along.

What Sebastian lacked in verbosity, he more than made up for as a horseman. He often bested Serena in speed, circling around with dancing eyes as she tried to catch up with him. A true gentleman wouldn't have made her feel inferior; he'd have given her a head start and perhaps even reined in his mount so she could end a race triumphant. But Sebastian was just a working class young man whom she didn't expect to observe niceties of the nobility.

One morning, Sebastian came alone. He apologized on behalf of his father, who had fallen ill from a rather unfortunate encounter with spoiled milk.

Serena watched agog as Sebastian spoke the longest sentence in their acquaintance.

"Would you like to cancel today's ride, Lady Serena?"

When she gathered her wits about her from his eloquence and the rich, deepening timbre of his voice, which pleased her ear very much, she said, "Of course, I don't mind. We won't go far. Crumpet simply needs exercising, or she'll sour for my next ride."

Their short ride turned rather long. They followed the contour of the coast before heading into thick forest, getting lost several times. Sebastian shocked her with ready conversation to keep her mind off their possible stranding, as though he had been waiting for this moment all his life.

He told her about his horses growing up, their quirks and funny mannerisms. She reciprocated by telling him about her first gelding and how she'd cried when he had to be put down for foundering. Stories flowed easily between them, and she wondered aloud why he hadn't said more to her around the others.

His intelligent brown eyes sought hers. "Papa said to not be familiar with the daughter of the house, so I took his advice to heart."

"I'm no daughter of the house," she retorted. "I'm simply Serena, who comes to the stables to ride the horses."

He pursed his lips, looking like he wanted to say more, and then just smiled.

When he did so, his eyes lit up. Serena held her breath, marveling at his beauty. She'd not yet come out, of course, so her experience with the opposite sex was very limited. But she was aware that in certain circles, say at the village dances, he would have girls fawning over him. And this thought upset her irrationally.

For the last leg of their journey back, she fell uncharacteristically quiet. She could sense him peering at her profile, wondering . . . she hoped he was wondering about her, anyway. Not that she would indulge his curiosity.

Heaven forbid that she would be attracted to the stable boy, but just in case, she poked around about his prospects.

"What do you dream to do someday, Sebastian?" she asked as they caught sight of the grand house.

"I am saving up my money so I can travel to America and get rich."

She gaped at him. He sounded so sure of himself. "Doing what?"

"Why, working with horses, of course. Horse breeding commands the highest prices there. Especially among the racing circles."

She believed him. The fox hunt brought out the rabid side of horse owners. They would pay obscene amounts of money for an intelligent and tried hunter.

Of course, she could not entertain notions of anything other than friendship between them. If that, even. Duke's daughters and stable hands could have nothing but a stiff formality between them.

Then why did she make sure, when they were coming upon the stables, that she observed a proper amount of distance from him—farther along and farther apart?

When, the next day, Sebastian was grooming her horse without his father, Serena stopped short at the stable door and watched. She should wait until later and bring her siblings. Other grooms could come with them.

But then he turned, flicking those brown eyes at her, and she forgot all those alternative plans. She took the reins of her horse and mounted like a proper lady, riding away from the grounds and across the knolls on the property. She spurred her horse to speed up and heard Sebastian's gelding coming upon her fast. Refusing to let up, she broke into a full gallop, laughing at the sensation of flight atop Crumpet.

By the time she came upon the dip in the pasture, she was too far gone to slow Crumpet. Her horse's leg got caught, sending Serena tumbling head over heels onto the grassy knoll.

She lay there stunned for a good minute, hearing Sebastian's horse thundering to her and him flinging himself onto the ground to skid to a stop beside her in a thrice. He lifted her head gingerly onto his lap as he tended to her. In a daze, she marveled that his eyes weren't actually a pure brown. They had specks of green in them, like the emerald hue of a tempest-tossed sea. Relief burned in them, and something else—a heat that spread through her body with sweet yearning.

"Are you all right?" he asked, his voice husky. Strained with worry.

Her lip twitched. His lap felt warm and safe. "I'm wonderful."

And then she remembered. "Crumpet!"

Her horse lay on her side on the carpet of green, whinnying pitifully. Serena wept over her horse's neck, willing the events of the day to rearrange themselves so that this last portion would be scratched off the sands of time.

Sebastian palpated Crumpet's foreleg. "It looks like she's simply gone lame. Hopefully, with some rest, she'll recover."

Serena wanted to believe him as she wiped away her tears.

"We must go back, Lady Serena," Sebastian said, helping her to her feet. "Let's go get the others."

She didn't object to him lifting her at the waist so she sat in front of him on his horse. Her arms circled his torso as she clung to him and sobbed against his shirt, soaking it, but he didn't seem to mind.

When they came to the stables, the others swarmed around them, including Sebastian's father. A look passed between father and son, inscrutable to her in her deep distress.

Serena would have wanted to see to Crumpet, but Jonathan prevailed upon her to stay. They would make sure that Crumpet would be treated with dignity.

"You're not killing her!" she protested.

Again, the father and son exchanged glances. "It depends how she's doing, my lady."

"I'm going with you."

Jonathan didn't look pleased, but he could not very well say no.

She watched the head groom and his son lead two other under-grooms out the direction they'd been earlier, a flintlock slung over the under-grooms' shoulders. She was glad she was coming. If they needed to put her horse down, she wanted to be able to ascertain it was absolutely necessary.

Several minutes later, they reached Crumpet. Jonathan coaxed her up, and she stood. Serena could have wept with joy. Perhaps not all was lost.

Crumpet put weight on the injured hoof and took a step. And another step. Until she was moving somewhat easily. Overjoyed, Serena turned to Sebastian with shining eyes. He stared at her for one long moment, his expression one she could not comprehend, and smiled.

Upon their return to the estate, her father called her into his library.

"I'm sorry to hear that your horse was injured," the Duke of Delaval said.

She beamed. "She will be better soon, I'm sure."

Papa drummed his fingers on his desk. "Someone said you rode back in the arms of the stable boy."

She gazed past his shoulder out at the expanse of their manicured gardens. Somewhere to the right, out of sight, stood the stables. And Sebastian. She returned her gaze to her father's. "Crumpet was injured. We had to share his horse."

The duke regarded her somberly. "Yes, I can see that. But from now on, you are not to ride with him again unchaperoned, understand?"

She wanted to ask him why, so he could put into words her confusion at the changes that seemed to be happening so fast. And yet she knew, in her heart of hearts, why. She may have only been fourteen, but her woman's instincts were already formed.

It didn't matter for a while, anyway. She couldn't muster up the interest to ride anyone else. A month later, with Crumpet back to being herself, Serena returned to the stables. Sebastian had retreated to his proper place as stable boy.

Just as Serena did, as the duke's daughter.

Two

Four years later, December 1800

"Will you be joining the fox hunt on Boxing Day?" Sebastian's father asked about the twenty-sixth of December. "His Grace has requested me to fill the staff."

Sebastian raised his head and considered his question. It was early December, an unusually cold and bitter winter in all of England, but particularly in the coastal parish where Leitham Park was situated. For horsemen whose work revolved mainly around the stables and outdoors, it felt good to be indoors, drinking a hearty glass of ale after supper.

Sebastian set his tankard down. "I haven't decided yet."

Father eyed him. "And what, pray, does your decision hinge upon?"

He could answer honestly—that he didn't want to be around Lady Serena and her succession of wealthy suitors—but he knew better. "I've been asked to join the hunting staff at Melton."

Father grunted. "Turning your head, are they? Mind the hand that feeds you."

"I do." Sebastian bristled.

"Is this about the money?"

"No. They're offering me less."

"Then why on earth are you considering such an offer?"

Sebastian tried to keep his voice even. "Father, you know very well that a good connection in horse circles could spell the success of my horse-breeding business."

"Do you still have it in your head to save up and go to America?"

Sebastian's stomach sank at his father's derisive attitude. "Yes."

Father's expression tightened. "I don't mind you pursuing anything there, but I'm getting on in years. I had been hoping that you could stay around for your mum and siblings."

"Understood." Sebastian stood and crossed over to the fireplace. "And I wish I could. It's a constant worry for me, for sure."

"Son, I know how important it is for you to be wealthy—"

"It's beyond money, Father," Sebastian interjected. "It's about improving our lot in life."

"Our lot in life! Why, it's as good as it gets. Head groom on a ducal estate."

"Good for you, Father. But that wouldn't be enough for me."

Father pinned him with his gaze. "Is it about her ladyship?"

Sebastian's breath stilled. He studied the dark paneling in the home that hadn't been truly their own since Father took on the job as head groom for the Duke of Delaval. The fire crackled in the grates, its merry movement one that didn't match how he felt at that moment. His unrequited love for

Lady Serena cast its ugly shadow across his heart, and he wished his father wouldn't have brought it up.

"Father, all that is in the past." His lie felt slick on his tongue.

"Is it? I saw you the other day, watching her—"

Sebastian cried, "Let it be, I beg of you."

Father nodded, his lips pressed tightly together. "Just a cautionary word, son. If you think you cannot contain your feelings for her, then perhaps it's time for you to move on to a different estate. I'm sure the ones in Melton are looking. I won't have you jeopardize our standing with His Grace."

Sebastian turned his heated gaze upon his father. "Are you truly asking me to leave your employ?"

"That's where I'm torn. You are an amazing horseman, and I couldn't be prouder of you. But your heart is rebellious and may bring us down."

"I am doing my best under the circumstances, Father."

"I believe that to be the truth. But a father's entitled to his worries."

"I have been conducting myself carefully, don't worry. I didn't realize I had compromised myself recently."

"You haven't, truly," Father acknowledged. "It may be that I am a good judge of people's motivations, though your mother likes to remind me that I seldom am." He grinned.

Sebastian's chest loosened at his father's lighter tone. "Mother is the best judge of character. You give yourself far too much credit reading my motivations."

Father's gaze did not waver. "I certainly hope so," he murmured. "I still blame myself for being sick those two days. Had I stayed healthy, you wouldn't be in this quandary . . . falling in love with the daughter of the house!"

Sebastian thought of the Lady Serena. That smooth skin, those sculpted cheekbones, and a mouth made for kissing. His wayward thoughts flooded him with guilt. She deserved his respect. She had been nothing but kind to him since his arrival at the estate, even with the discomfort of their mutual infatuation cut short.

If only she didn't share his passion for horses. In his dreams, they flew on beautiful mounts together, in a world where neither rank nor income mattered.

That was why America held so much fascination for him. In America, one could forge one's own success by his own hand.

Sebastian shook his head. "It was through no fault of yours."

Father set down his drink and got to his feet. He was not a big man, and he walked with a limp from a wayward horse that chose to kick at his trainer. But his manner was imposing, commanding respect not just from his employees but also his firstborn son.

"I would think so. Still, I made it far too easy for two young, susceptible people to get too close. Very well, we shall speak no more of it, seeing that you seem to be cured of your unhealthy obsession. Mind that you do not forget to check on our ailing Stepper tonight."

"I won't."

Father's words left Sebastian wanting after his footsteps echoed faintly into silence. He stared into the fire, wishing that his father's hope he was "cured" was true. As the years passed, and as Lady Serena's beauty grew, so did Sebastian's secret love for her increase.

Sebastian put on layers quickly for the weather outside. He strode out, his face freezing in the wind. It would feel good to enter the barn, in the warmth and company of the horses. The stables served as his first home, ever since he could ride astride.

With a lantern in hand, he walked across the grounds, his boots crunching the veneer of ice that formed on the path to the barn. It was hardly a barn, but a behemoth, housing over thirty horses this hunting season. It was a full-time occupation for Sebastian as under-groom at any rate, keeping the duke's horses ridden and the greenhorns trained for the upcoming fox hunt.

He lifted his eyes to the building and paused. A light flickered behind its closed doors. Surely, none of the stable hands was foolish enough to leave a lamp on inside. So who could possibly be here this time of night?

Opening the doors, Sebastian inserted himself inside to avoid the icy chill. But the chill continued in his heart when he saw the slim figure standing with lamp in hand by Stepper's stall.

"Lady Serena," he breathed.

She turned, startled. It was a blessing she didn't drop the lantern, as surprised as she looked. "Sebastian!" She lifted her hand to her woolen scarf. "You scared me."

"I apologize." He averted his gaze. "I can return later."

"No, don't." Her eyes glimmered in the lamplight. "I don't want to inconvenience you. I am the one who must leave. I don't wish to get in your way. I was merely checking on our friend here."

"Let me assure you, you won't be in my way. Having you here is probably calming to him."

She certainly wasn't calming to him. His mind raced, thinking back to the conversation he had just had with his father. Avoiding Lady Serena at all costs, indeed. He should run off, and return later—it was probably the most prudent move. But if he did so, he would signal that she still affected him. And he didn't want to make her feel any more uncomfortable than they'd been in their younger years.

Sebastian kept his face averted as he approached the stall. The red roan snorted his welcome, even as his eyes reflected the pain of a torn muscle on his right foreleg.

Bringing back a recollection of a lame Crumpet four years ago. And other . . . memories.

Crumpet was now one of the seasoned hunters, while the younger Stepper seemed to find favor with Lady Serena. She had taken on training him until this last mishap.

“If you don’t mind,” she said, “I’ll watch.”

“Of course, I don’t mind what your ladyship does. I’ll just be about, checking on his dressing.”

As it turned out, going about his business of tending to a horse was difficult with a beautiful lady looking on. Especially a beautiful lady who shouldn’t have captured his heart in the first place. He hung his lamp on a hook and proceeded to check the horse, trying to pretend a calm he did not feel.

“Will you be at the fox hunt on Boxing Day?” she asked.

He smiled but didn’t answer right away.

She cocked her head. “What is so amusing?”

“You’re the second person who’s asked me that today.” He glanced up and was captivated by the radiance of her countenance brought on by her smile. He forced himself to look back down at his task.

“And who was the first?”

“My father.”

“What was your answer?”

“I told him I was thinking about it.”

“Oh? You’ve never missed in the past, why would you now?”

Sebastian lifted Stepper’s leg and ran his hand over the swelling along the knee. Thankfully, it had gone down. He straightened up slowly and faced Lady Serena. “I’ve been asked to help at a drag in Melton.”

Her face fell, before she made an attempt at a smile. "I can't blame them. I would, too, if I were running a hunt. I'm sure Papa will miss you, though."

"He may have to get used to me being gone. I have already been making plans for a voyage to America next year, once winter thaws."

She gaped at him. "That's news to me. So . . ." Her voice cooled. "You've fixed a date."

"Please." He took a step toward her. "You mustn't tell anyone. You're the first to know."

Her beautiful blue eyes, fringed with thick lashes, gazed at him solemnly. "I'm honored you would tell me."

Did he sense a trace of sarcasm in her words? Her lovely mouth turned down at the ends, and she looked at her gloved hands.

"I didn't think you'd care," he murmured.

She raised her eyes to his, allowing him to look inside her soul. He didn't dare hope. Didn't dare think. But somewhere in their shining depths, there was yearning.

Just as quickly, she returned her gaze to the floor, littered with straw. "I thought we were friends."

Her plaintive words squeezed his heart. *Friends.* Was that how she looked upon him? "I can hardly expect your friendship."

She raised her eyes to his. "Do you paint me to be such a cruel taskmistress?"

He shook his head. "No, not that."

"Then why did you not tell me sooner?"

"Because then I'd have had to acknowledge that I was leaving." That was all he had courage to say. His gaze grazed her mouth, trembling with emotion. "I would think you'd be rejoicing."

"Why would I?"

"I no longer have to torment you with my ill-humor." Sebastian closed his eyes, then opened them again. "Forgive me. I am being far too familiar with your ladyship."

Her gaze faltered. "I had hoped you would keep me posted on your dream. You had confided in me, once." She took a deep breath and looked past him to Stepper. "How is he?"

Back to safer topics, Sebastian gave his report with a frisson of relief, even as he was still aware of Lady Serena's closeness, just a mere two arm-lengths away. Alone with him in this enclosed barn, walling off the rest of the world.

"The swelling is down, which is good to see."

"Will he be rideable at the hunt?"

"I would recommend that he not be used. But maybe he will be better by then, who knows?"

"I would hope so. I wanted to ride him."

"Someone as light as you shouldn't pose a problem. But he might step wrong, and the results could be devastating."

"Of course. I understand. I can always use good ol' Crumpet." She paused. "Sebastian . . ."

He flicked a glance at her, trapped in her soft expression.

"It's your business, of course, what you do for your work. But I had hoped you would stay on." Her eyes shone with affection. "Good night."

Sebastian's brain refused to function, and he could only stand there like a numbskull. Lady Serena stepped back and away, taking her light and warmth with her out of the barn. He wished he could have talked to her more, about his dreams and plans.

About hers.

That would have been presumptuous of him, of course. Best to keep his thoughts and feelings to himself. Best to shut his heart to her forever. Even if he were to make his money and return, her father would never entertain a suit from a former stable boy. However grand and rich he got.

Three

Serena's heartbeat returned to somewhat normal after entering the main house.

She had gone to the stables on impulse to check on Stepper. All right . . . if she were to be honest to herself, she had hoped to "accidentally" come upon Sebastian. She was a fool, she knew it, holding a torch for this man in her dreams. They couldn't have a future together, and yet she continued to yearn for him. She persisted on sizing up all her suitors in terms of their riding prowess. Which, of course, could not even be close to mirroring Sebastian's.

Since Crumpet's accident, Sebastian had been respectful toward her, not giving anyone reason to doubt that his loyalty lay with his employer, the duke. Making Serena both frustrated and amazed.

Mostly frustrated.

In the hallway, the housekeeper ran into her and looked astonished. "Has my lady been outside in the cold? You look positively frozen."

"Yes, I was, checking on a horse. Would you be so kind as to ring for tea?"

"Right away, my lady. There's already been a summons from your brother. He just got in himself."

"He did?" Serena's stomach clenched at the thought of Quinn.

"Would you like me to serve your tea in the green room? That's where he's at."

Serena hesitated. At twenty-four, Quinn acted irresponsibly with his time and money. Although older than Serena, he was not necessarily wiser. He had a gambling problem and had been a source of worry for the family. Somehow, he managed to stay in his father's good graces. Perhaps solely from his birth order in the family.

Last she'd heard, he had vowed to stay away this Christmas. The fact he had returned so early didn't bode well. It meant one of two things. He either had run out of money, or he was being hounded by debtors. Or both.

"In the green room is fine, Mrs. Renfrew," Serena told the housekeeper.

Mrs. Renfrew bustled about on her errand as Serena started taking off her winter outercoat, making her way down to the green room.

At the doors, she paused. Quinn wasn't alone. Papa's voice enunciated the following words, alarming Serena: "You are not to sell Stepper."

Serena pressed closer to the door, knowing she shouldn't eavesdrop, but wanting to hear their candid conversation.

"Why ever not, Papa?" Quinn's wheedling voice grated on Serena's nerves. "He's a good piece of horseflesh."

"Is that all he is to you?" Serena could picture Papa's eyebrows rising.

"Of course, not," Quinn replied. "But I know for a fact that he was sired with high hopes for his value in the future. You'd gotten him for my purposes, as I recall."

"It was with the understanding that you were to use him as a hunter, and not as a mere speculative pawn. Your sister happens to like him—"

"She likes *all* the horses, Papa. Even the worthless ones."

"And which would those be?" Papa's voice was quiet.

"The ones who have never won the races, the ones with sad prospects. The ones prone to injury, like Stepper."

"You wouldn't recognize quality horseflesh if it kicked you in the rear. I'm done with this conversation. If Serena says she agrees to sell him, then I will possibly re-consider."

Papa's footsteps sounded heavy and close. Serena retreated a few steps away from the door and pretended to be entering the room just then.

"Good evening, Papa," she said, dipping into a curtsy.

"Good evening." He glanced at her clothes. "Where have you been?"

"I was in the stables, checking on Stepper."

An approving light gleamed in Papa's eyes. "Very good. I am glad to see my daughter carry on with my love for horses." He glanced back into the open doorway, where Quinn watched with a frustrated expression. "Unlike some of my offspring."

Papa went down the hallway while Serena entered the room with trepidation, much like how a traveler would approach a nest of vipers.

"What brings you back to Leitham Park, brother?" Serena asked, keeping a light tone.

"If you must know, I lost heavily at White's."

She snorted. "So now you wish to put in a good day's work and earn your keep?"

"Very funny." A speculative gleam entered his eye. "I am glad to see you, my dearest sister." He came forward and kissed the air beside her cheeks. "I was just thinking of you."

"Oh?"

"Papa is under the delusion that Stepper is worth more than he purchased him for. I heard that he had gone lame. His value will only continue to plummet in his condition. Especially if he is used at the hunt. We all know how hard that could be on our hunters."

Serena gave him a flinty gaze. "Sebastian recommends that we don't use him."

"Sebastian?"

"Our head groom's son. He is a groom to his father this season."

Quinn raised an eyebrow. "You will put stock into this . . . this *nobody's* words?"

"He is not a nobody," she retorted hotly.

"Well, well." Malice crept into Quinn's eyes. "Perhaps to the world, but not to my dear sister."

"I don't know what you're talking about."

He mimicked her. "I had an inkling at one time, that you set your cap upon this fellow, but it was too preposterous to even believe that. But now, thinking on it, and colored by my worldly experience, I realize now that he has caught your eye."

"Don't be ridiculous, Quinn." Heat crept under Serena's neck.

"That's right. He's only a stable boy."

"He is *not* just a stable boy. He is . . ."

Her words trailed at the triumph in Quinn's eyes. He had baited her, and she had fallen straight for his trap. She pressed her lips together and crossed her arms over her chest.

Quinn may have been a fool at times, but tonight, he assessed her shrewdly. "Were you at the stables tonight?"

"Yes," came her terse reply.

Realization dawned in his eyes. "With that stable boy?"

Her cheeks warmed. "I was visiting Stepper when Sebastian came in, too."

"What a coincidence."

Serena's fists curled at her sides. "I had hoped to join you for tea, but I have to plead a headache."

"How convenient. Too bad." Quinn's lip curled. "I suppose I can at least give you some words of wisdom."

She had already turned, and looked back at him slowly.

His eyes turned to flint. "If you do not allow me to sell Stepper, you might want to make sure that Papa doesn't catch drift of this infatuation of yours."

"Or what?"

"Did I imply a threat?"

"Your tone suggested it."

He cast over a wolfish grin. "Then you might want to be careful with any dalliances with that stable boy. Papa will be sure to marry you off or send you away over a whiff of scandal."

"How dare you."

"I've seen him. Strapping young man. I wouldn't put it past a duke's daughter to lose her head over him."

Serena marched out of the drawing room, trying to keep shreds of her pride intact. Why must everyone act as though she was in love with Sebastian?

She had long accepted her fate that she could never have him. But even as she told herself thus, she recalled watching him gently checking Stepper's leg and his self-deprecating humor. Qualities she valued in a man.

How she wished she could cross the line dividing them.

Quinn's threat rang empty. She had no fear of indiscretion, and she trusted Sebastian to exercise similar restraint. Hadn't he done so, over the years, even though she had practically flung herself in his path at every subconscious turn?

As she thought of Quinn's avarice, anger flared within her. She would never allow the sale of Stepper to a careless buyer. She knew the kind of "friends" Quinn ran around with, and they cared nothing for the animal, just his equivalent in gold coins.

As for this matter over Sebastian, she would put it to rest once and for all. Papa brought together the most eligible bachelors to the fox hunt. Serena would take her pick and banish Sebastian completely out of her mind . . . and heart.

Four

The fox hunt at Leitham Park had earned a well-deserved reputation. Apart from the draw of the beautiful grounds overlooking the cliffs at Derryshire, the hunters and hounds were of impeccable breeding—Sebastian made sure of that.

Even at his age of twenty, younger than most breeders of respectable note, Sebastian didn't bear false modesty. He knew he did good work, and every horse under his training at least tripled in value. As his father's apprentice, he ran excellent stables for the duke and a vigorous fox hunt that was the envy of all the ton.

Then why was he dithering on Boxing Day, worried that he'd let His Grace down?

Because by helping with this fox hunt, he wasn't staying away from Lady Serena like he should.

He'd tried everything, heaven knew. He avoided her during her regular rides. He assigned others to chores related to her horses. And he even forbade himself to allow his gaze to linger on her as she confidently modeled the latest riding fashion. But the fox hunt was a different beast. They would be forced to come into close contact with each other, simply by the fact they were both aggressive riders, easily breaking ahead of the pack.

Shaking his head, he went about his duties, supervising the handling of the hounds who milled about in a dense pack. They barked as they sensed the excitement in the air.

Spectators in landaus and carriages arrived, as did the nobility and the well-connected in their fancy attire. A few ladies joined in the fray, planning to watch from the sidelines or ride, but not roughshod like the rest of them—Lady Serena excluded. She would run the hunt with the hunters, and jump like everyone else. His Grace permitted his oldest daughter that exception, mayhap even encouraged it. Lord Quinn mostly gambled on horses nowadays, and had a weak seat.

At the thought of Lady Serena riding in the hunt, Sebastian shook his head. She was a marvel to behold. When in her element and cutting an elegant figure in her riding habit and winter coat, he could hardly be expected to resist a glance.

He knew better, however. He would have to keep his distance.

It shouldn't be an issue; he would be busy starting at eleven o'clock, when the master of the hunt was expected to blow his horn to signal the start.

It was a cold, dreary day, with a fog rolling from the coast and casting frost on all it touched. And yet there was something magical about the wintry scene. And it was the perfect day for a hunt. With visibility low, he expected a challenge traversing the course; it was a level of difficulty that Sebastian relished. He would assist the riders before the hunt, but while on it, he was also one of them. Whatever needed to be done, he would help with, though someone else was tasked with keeping the hounds in line and focused. A different team of riders would take care of any injured animals or riders. If a spill were to happen, the hunt would go on.

With the sun peeping through gray clouds, optimism buoyed Sebastian's spirits. Until he saw the small group—some half-dozen dandies—surrounding Lady Serena and her riding friends.

He wasn't one to judge based on pompous looks, but it was hard to ignore the preoccupation of one particular gentleman upon his cravat remaining tied properly. Ian Sutton, the Earl of Winthrop, committed the gravest of these vain obsessions.

"Lady Serena," Winthrop said, bowing at the waist atop his chestnut. "The hunt is made even brighter by your presence this morning."

"Is it?" She peered at his face. "Are you sure you aren't merely affected still by last night's cups?"

His friends tittered.

"I assure you, no," Winthrop said. "I deliberately stayed away from the gaming halls last night so that I could be fresh and alert this morning. I wouldn't want to be left in the dust."

"I'm glad to hear that," she said amiably. "We wouldn't want you to fall and break your . . . cravat now, would we?"

More tittering.

Winthrop turned an embarrassed shade of pink. "I had hoped you had forgotten last year's fall, but alas, I see that it's still fresh on your mind."

"I won't hold it against you," Lady Serena said, turning her horse away to join her lady friends. She looked over her shoulder. "So long as you ride like a sport and not try to cross my path when I best you."

She didn't see the dark look that passed over Winthrop's face, nor the mutterings he exchanged with his friends. They were blackguards as far as Sebastian was concerned. He would pay them particular mind. Much could happen in the chaos of a hunt, giving cover to anyone wanting to do someone harm. He wouldn't put anything past this spoiled aristocrat. For good measure, Sebastian decided he would put himself between the buck and Lady Serena.

The master of the hunt sounded the horn, the hounds were let loose, and everyone followed them in a pillion through the path that spread out into the fields of the estate. The fog continued to roll, lending an eerie atmosphere to the hunt. With the hounds baying, the day almost seemed to be held in homage of a pagan ritual. Sebastian supposed fox hunting was steeped in ritual, but was more civilized than that.

Clods of dirt and grass flew under hoof. He kept an eye on the hounds and nipped some bad behavior and distractions here and there.

As the horses began moving, Sebastian ended up riding alongside Lady Serena.

The broadest grin spread across his face. He couldn't help it—with the cold winter wind cutting at his face and trying to permeate his wool coat, he was happiest at the fox hunt.

Her smile mirrored his exultant feeling.

Now they were riding neck and neck. The hounds had caught scent of the fox, even though they hadn't actually caught sight of him.

The air was wet with a drizzle, little pinpricks that pummeled Sebastian's face. As the ride progressed, however, the cold no longer nipped. His body warmed from the exertion, and even the sun peeked from behind the clouds.

Lady Serena sailed over a hedge. Upon her graceful landing, she looked over her shoulder at Sebastian. He followed, his mount's powerful legs extending strong and sure into the mud. He could sense the iciness under his horse's hooves, but he was able to wrest control of him right away.

For the next few minutes, they jumped over fences and tromped over streams. Their horses' hooves dug into the mud. The clouds covered the sun once again, and fog thickened.

It pleased Sebastian that Winthrop and his friends had dropped back in the hunt. There were the master and a few stalwarts up ahead, and then there were Sebastian and Lady Serena. Her lady friends had also fallen behind with the rest of the pack.

Coming up was the greatest obstacle yet. A fallen log that only came into sight as they approached the copse. It had a wide diameter, the size of a barrel, and there were scraggly branches that could snag even the most careful rider.

Sebastian wanted to call out in warning to Lady Serena, but he bit his tongue. She was an experienced rider. She would ride this out. As he predicted, she collected her horse and sailed over the obstacle. He held his breath as he watched her horse kick out its hindlegs, its forelegs landing in front of the log.

Her beaming smile said it all.

Sebastian stared at her beautiful face, transfixed. He knew then that he had told himself a brazen lie.

He still loved her. Most ardently.

And if he had to chase her to the ends of the earth to win her love, he would.

Five

Serena returned to the grand house in complete disarray. Twigs littered her hair, askew under her hat. Mud splattered her scarlet coat. Ice caked her boots.

She didn't care.

Joy filled her heart, especially at the memory of running the hunt alongside Sebastian.

For all of everyone's effort, they didn't catch the fox. That was never of prime importance to Serena. In the past, the failure of a hunt filled her with frustration, for what was the point? But then her father never seemed to care as well. He taught her that the hunt was more than just about catching their prey. It was about good horsemanship, being one with your mount, and enjoying the beauty of Leitham Park.

She had ridden a different horse, as Sebastian recommended, since Stepper was not yet in good shape for the rigors of all that jumping. She'd chosen a lanky young gelding named Rondo whom Papa had bought from a Spanish trader, and he had performed nicely.

Through her toilette for that evening's festivities, Serena let her mind wander back to her ride alongside Sebastian. She had vowed to not act on their mutual attraction, but no one could curtail her imagination. How well he had filled out his wool riding coat, looking every bit the nobleman, just like Winthrop and his friends.

It was a shame Sebastian couldn't attend the ball tonight.

She'd have much preferred to continue to spend time at the stables, but she needed to do her duty. She wondered idly where Quinn had gone. He'd disappeared, it seemed, and was nowhere to be found at the hunt.

An orchestra played a lilting tune upon Serena's entrance into the ballroom that nearly rivaled that of Almack's with its numerous alcoves and grandiose length. Papa opened the fox hunt ball with a charming speech where he complimented Serena on her riding abilities and searched for Quinn fruitlessly in the crowd to commend him for . . . here, he trailed off to the titters of the crowd.

Soon, however, Quinn did appear, sporting a grin that filled Serena with unease. He looked like the olden days, when he'd play a prank on their governess and never got caught for it.

"Why the happy face, brother?" she asked as people paid their respects to them.

"Can't I smile for once? I feel free as a bird."

Serena gave him a sidelong glance. "Aren't you going to elaborate on your good fortune?"

"No, I will not." He smirked. "Suffice it to say it has nothing to do with gambling or women."

"That's good," Serena said, trying to tamp down the derision in her voice. When her brother was sincerely trying, he could be pleasant and amiable.

"Here's Winthrop." To the gentleman, Quinn said, "And how did you fare out on the fox hunt today, my friend? Did you keep your seat this time?"

Winthrop winced. Off the horse, he actually looked less pompous. Perhaps it had to do with the fact that he didn't have to look down upon others from that supercilious nose.

Serena regretted that she was too harsh on him. She made an effort to engage him in conversation. Until she noticed him preening in the mirrored pillar, so he could, once again, adjust his cravat.

She looked away, bored and unhopeful.

In the corner of her eye, she caught a glimpse of Jonathan, Sebastian's father. He appeared to be looking for Serena's father, and, finding him, leaned close into a whispered conversation. The duke's face paled. Those nearby glanced over, watching the interaction with interest. And then Papa walked ponderously across the ballroom. Serena excused herself from Winthrop and other men waiting to ask to dance with her and caught up with Papa as he neared a doorway.

"What is the matter, Papa?" Serena asked.

Papa's expression was grim. "Stepper has been stolen from right under Sebastian's watch."

Six

Sebastian's head hurt from where someone had hit him on the head. Memories seemed to come and go. He remembered vaguely that as he entered the barn after the hunt, someone hit him with a blunt object. That spot on the back of his head still smarted, and blood transferred to his fingers.

Father had come upon him before he regained consciousness. He had been lying on the cold stable floor for who knew how long. The verdict Father had laid out chilled him to the core: Stepper had been stolen!

Other stable hands were questioned, but no one had seen anything.

Where he sat conversing with Father, he could hear a lady's voice above the chaos and din of a stable settling in from a fox hunt, not to mention the horse thievery.

"I wish to see Sebastian," came Lady Serena's voice.

Sebastian tried to rise from the bench he had been sitting on, but Lady Serena motioned for him to stop. "You don't look well. Please stay seated." She nodded toward his father. "I was distraught to hear of this."

"It's an odd sort of thievery," Father said. "A brazen act in broad daylight."

"Not easily noticed while people were coming and going with their horses." She sighed and turned her attention to Sebastian. "Are you terribly hurt?"

"I received a blow to the head. The wound is still tender. However, I am recovering. Please do not be troubled by it, my lady."

She opened her mouth as though to speak, but closed it again. She looked out of sorts, her fingers kneading a handkerchief. "May I speak to both of you in confidence?"

"Of course."

Sebastian followed his father and Lady Serena into a quiet section of the barn, where she paced before speaking again.

"I believe I know who is behind this theft," she said.

Father swallowed visibly. "And who would that be, my lady?"

"My brother."

Despite feeling even more light-headed, Sebastian remained standing. "I wondered the same thing."

"He wasn't at the hunt today, like he normally is."

"Do you think he committed the thievery himself?"

"Of course, not." Lady Serena snorted in an unladylike fashion. "Quinn doesn't like to be troubled over horses. He'd just as soon waste his time in gambling dens."

"How could he possibly profit from a lame horse?" Father wondered aloud.

Lady Serena's lips tightened into a pained smile. "Stepper *had* been getting better. Even lame, he still has a lot of potential. Had he recovered fully, he would have fetched a good sum. Lord Quinn wanted me to sell him now, but I refused to give my approval. He only cares about money, not the welfare of the horse."

Sebastian frowned. "It still doesn't make sense. I don't understand why he would need to do this. Forgive me for being impertinent, but he has enough funds to keep him afloat for a while, does he not?"

"Not at the rate he's gambling, the wastrel." She looked away. "I hate it. I hate seeing him ruin his life. But at least in the past, he was simply ruining his. Now, he has dragged a horse into the mire, so to speak . . ."

The barn door, which had been slightly ajar, opened fully. Lord Quinn appeared, sending a chill into the room.

"I suspected I would find you here, sister," he said, his eyes roaming insolently over the two men. "The horse has returned."

Everyone gasped, looking at Quinn.

"I must see him." Lady Serena's eyes narrowed. "If he's been harmed in any way . . ."

"Must you look at me that way, sister? You appear to lay the blame at my feet."

"After our conversation, how could I not?"

Lady Serena dipped her head and flashed Sebastian a quick glance. He wished he could say something, to tell her that she had his sympathy, but of course, he didn't have the opportunity to do so in front of the others. She sailed out of the barn, her head held high.

"I must check on the horse," Father said. "I'll take your leave, Lord Quinn."

Sebastian would have followed, but Lord Quinn said, "A moment, Sebastian."

They were alone, Sebastian keeping his suspicion of this man in check.

In the ordinary circumstances of the stable, covered with straw and dust, Lord Quinn's coat appeared immaculate. Out of place. He straightened his cuffs. "My sister is under the delusion that when she says jump, we all jump."

Sebastian held his tongue. Certainly, no one could fault her for asserting her maturity over this man.

"As the events unfolded today, I have been in constant communication with my father. He has, for some time, been aware of your disloyalty to our stables—"

"Disloyalty!" Sebastian echoed.

"Do you deny that you plan to leave your employ as soon as you are able to scrounge around enough money for your passage to America?"

Sebastian's stomach plummeted. "No, I do not deny it. I am shocked, however, that a nobleman like you would care about what a lowly stable hand plans to do with his life."

"A stable hand who has turned a foolish lady's head."

Sebastian's heart pounded even as he kept his voice even. "And who would that be?"

Lord Quinn smirked. "Lady Serena."

"You malign your sister's good name."

"Do I?" Lord Quinn raised an eyebrow. "It is obvious to all who observe—she has not been very cooperative with her suitors. So many men vying for her hand in marriage, and yet she does not appear to have any interest, whatsoever. You have bewitched her. So much so, she even gave you due credit for advising her about Stepper."

"So that is what this is all about," Sebastian returned hotly. "You wish to control every aspect of your sister's life."

"So long as she doesn't control mine." Lord Quinn's eyes gleamed. "Whatever it takes. With that, I have the pleasure of informing you that we are letting you go."

The words bounced in Sebastian's head.

"On what grounds?" he said, his voice lowering to a growl.

"You had one job, Sebastian Bromley, and you proved your incompetence. His Grace no longer wishes to entrust his stable of horses to you and your father."

Not Father, too! Sebastian's fists curled at his side. This was unconscionable. Lord Quinn was already leaving. Sebastian wanted to pull his shoulder back and punch the man in the nose.

"My father is the best head groom your family has ever had, and you know it."

Lord Quinn's lip curled. "I did. But I cannot see how he can continue working here when you've been let go. I don't think it will make for a good working environment for the rest of the stable staff." His smile didn't reach his eyes. "I'm sure His Grace will agree."

Lady Serena had returned during the tail end of the exchange, and now she approached her brother. "What trouble are you stirring up now, Quinn?"

Lord Quinn held her arm. "Nothing that should concern you, my dear. Sebastian has been sacked, and his father will be, too."

Lady Serena's shocked gaze, with its apology, skittered down to where Sebastian stood.

"Quinn, you are making a grave mistake. We mustn't—"

Lord Quinn didn't let her go. "Come along. You've wreaked enough havoc here."

A light went out of her eyes, and she let him lead her away.

In the end, His Grace kept Jonathan Bromley in his employ. Father tried to make heads and tails of it all, but in the end, he could only express his frustrations privately.

"You'll be able to get a good job at another grand house, I'm sure," Father said.

"We shall see," was all Sebastian replied.

Sebastian somehow found the strength to pack his belongings, staring at the bare walls which had been his home for the past four years.

He'd given over four good years of his life, heart and soul, to this job. He'd learned so much, and he thought he could give a little bit more until the next stage of his life.

It wasn't meant to be.

He imagined Lady Serena's stricken face. Did she truly feel concern for him, or just for the welfare of the animals?

Exhaling deeply, he shook his head. He was allowing Lord Quinn to poison the good he had experienced working for the Duke of Delaval. It was hard not to, though, under the circumstances.

The older Bromley met Sebastian outside the living quarters. "I don't understand," Father said, looking bewildered. "What did you do to incur his ire?"

Other than love his sister from afar?

"I don't know, Father," Sebastian said, truthfully. "I don't know."

Seven

Serena was far from serene returning to that night's ball, one of the many that would be held on occasion of the hunt. She stayed on the sidelines with her riding friends Amelie and Jenny, the daughters of an earl and a marquis, respectively. They were trying to rouse her spirits.

"Why the long face, Serena?" Amelie asked, her blue eyes dancing. "Today, of all days? You are usually so carefree. A day trailing a fox on the hunt always does that to you."

Serena sighed. "This wasn't your typical fox hunt."

Jenny leaned toward Amelie. "Amelie, must you be so insensitive? One of her horses was stolen. I cannot imagine if my beloved animal were to disappear."

"But hasn't he been found?" Amelie asked.

"Yes, he has." Serena gazed out into the crowded ballroom with unseeing eyes.

"Then why are you still terribly sad?"

Serena thought of Sebastian, and guilt assailed her once again. Quinn's petty grievances had gone too far, but Serena had brought the devastation on Sebastian. If only she hadn't mentioned Sebastian by name when she discussed Stepper with Quinn, perhaps he would have been able to stay on. Just a few more months until he left for America.

But now she wouldn't even see him again.

"I'm not terribly sad," Serena lied, forcing herself to smile.

"Good." Jenny tapped her lightly with her fan. "Because Winthrop is coming this way."

Serena focused her distracted mind upon Ian Sutton, Earl of Winthrop. She noted how handsome he looked in his well-cut coat and immaculately tied cravat. If she were to settle for someone, it might as well be someone as debonair as him.

"May I have the pleasure of this dance?" he asked, offering his arm.

She bowed, accepting his arm. She hoped to feel sparks.

He led her to the floor, where she did her best to be amiable and answer his polite inquiries correctly, and danced the proper steps to the music. Lord Ian was an accomplished dancer, much more so than a horse rider.

Serena chastised herself for the unfair comparison even as she imagined Sebastian. How courageous he had been in the saddle, riding at breakneck speed alongside her at the hunt.

She wondered if he had already left the estate.

At the end of their set, Lord Ian escorted Serena back to her friends. She partnered with others a few more times, lively performances all, lifting her heavy heart and her spirits. Toward the end of the evening, she had almost succeeded in banishing Sebastian from her mind.

And then Lord Ian hinted at something that mostly worried her.

"It would be a great honor if you would take a drive with me tomorrow, Lady Serena."

Serena certainly had no earthly reason why she shouldn't accept his invitation.

But when morning came around and an icy rain fell, she received a note from Lord Ian that due to the weather, he would have to postpone his visit. Which was perfectly fine with Serena. She glanced at the message with relief, before watching listlessly out her window as the gray day continued with steady rain.

She didn't even have the escape that riding provided. Her younger sisters entered then—Margaret and Olivia, two bright spots of sunshine in her life at that moment. Margaret was twelve and Olivia ten. Both of them chatterboxes.

"Mama needed to rest," Margaret reported, "so both Livvy and I were sent by Miss Linsdown to torment someone else."

"I doubt that's what your governess said," Serena tut-tutted.

"That's exactly what she said," Livvy piped up, "and I suggested you."

Serena was a sport and indulged them in some parlor games until all three girls were giggling together. Miss Linsdown poked her head in and rounded up her charges for their lessons.

"But I thought we were on holiday!" Livvy protested. "Must we go back to our studies so soon?"

Miss Linsdown confirmed this, leaving Serena to herself for the moment. A maid came and informed her that Her Grace wanted to speak to her.

In one of the loveliest rooms in the house, Mama was reclining on her sofa with a blanket over her lap, with Papa hovering over her. He straightened up at Serena's entrance, gave her an uneasy glance, and excused himself. Serena stared at his retreating figure until he disappeared. They hadn't talked about the fox hunt nor his dismissal of Sebastian. Somehow, Serena suspected that he wouldn't take kindly to her probing.

Serena walked across the room, sat on the sofa, and held her mother's hands. Catherine, Duchess of Delaval, still showed traces of beauty on her illness-ravaged frame. Her cheeks were gaunt, and her skin appeared translucent, but her eyes still sparkled with life.

"And how is my darling daughter today?"

Serena mulled the possibility of telling her mother a gentler version of the events of the past days. It would be for the best.

"A bit gloomy, like the weather," was all she said.

"Fustian. You must not allow yourself to be affected by this abominable weather. You and I know very well that if you do, you will be dark and dismal the rest of your life."

Serena smiled, even though inside, she ached.

Mama searched her eyes. "Ah, but it's true. You are sad."

"Perhaps a little," Serena said, turning at the waist to brush away a tear.

Mama opened her arms, and Serena leaned in for a hug without further invitation. Mama was frail, but her touch felt strong. Steadfast.

"My dearest daughter, please tell me why you're unhappy."

Serena hesitated. "So long as you promise me that you will not tell a living soul."

"Of course." Mama settled on her pillow to watch Serena.

"I am in love with someone completely inappropriate." There. She said it. There was no turning back. Her heart beat quickly, and her palms turned clammy, but it felt good to finally unburden her secret to someone.

Mama blinked rapidly. "But how did that happen?"

"It all began when I was fourteen and we hired his father as head groom." Serena traced a pattern on the settee with her rounded fingernail. "He brought his son Sebastian then."

Mama watched her with a steady gaze. In the depths of her eyes, Serena could see her mother was no fool. She could see right through her.

"I know of him, of course. He made an impression on you?"

Serena nodded. "He was a kindred spirit. We both love horses."

"As I did, in my younger days. That's what attracted me to your father." Mama paused. "Continue."

"When his father took ill for two days, I went out to ride with Sebastian. I didn't mean to fall in love—"

"But you did."

Serena lowered her head. "I've fought those feelings since. I knew a deeper friendship could amount to nothing. Over the years, we both have kept our distance, honestly. Still, in the stables, we rode and trained horses within sight of each other. And I . . . I thought I'd be cured, only to find myself admiring him further."

"From the window, I have seen him training the horses. He is an impressive horseman."

"He is." Serena's wistful smile quickly disappeared. "But Quinn has reared his ugly head and has been needling me about what he called my inappropriate relationship with Sebastian. Not only that, but Quinn decided to target him with his vitriol. Yesterday, Quinn talked Papa into letting Sebastian go."

"Oh dear." Mama's hands fluttered helplessly around her neck. "Why would he do that?"

"Because I didn't want to give my blessing to sell one of

the horses upon Sebastian's advice, and I said so. Quinn, I'm sure, arranged for Sebastian's dismissal out of spite."

"I do worry about your brother," Mama murmured. "So . . . this Sebastian. Do you still hold a candle for him?"

"No. I mustn't, anyway." Serena hung her head. "I've ruined his life enough. I honestly have come to peace about him. I never entertained notions that we could have a future together."

Mama smiled faintly. "I hear that the Earl of Winthrop has piqued your interest."

Serena stared at her mother in surprise. "How do you hear about all this?"

"I have my ways." Mama's eyes twinkled. "My maids are dutiful . . . and very entertaining."

"I can imagine," Serena said in a dry tone. "I don't mind, Mama. Here you are cooped up, and I don't even take the time to visit you as often as I could."

"I'm often asleep. Can I blame you?" Mama's eyes drifted to the window. "My only regret is that I can no longer join you in boxing up our things to give them to the needy in our parish."

Serena's heart ached for Mother. "I could arrange to have everything brought up here, Mother, so you could still participate."

Mama's eyes lit up. "That would be wonderful. I'd also heard of a home for orphans in the next parish over. Perhaps you can extend a visit there, too?"

"You can count on me to do so, Mama."

"As for your problem—"

"It's all right," Serena assured her. "I just needed a listening ear. Thank you."

"Of course." Mama smiled. "Perhaps today you can play

the piano? A soothing melody would do much to lighten my spirits."

"I would be happy to."

Serena proceeded to play a sweet melody she'd learned just the year before. It had a series of delightful trills that she took pride in being able to do on the instrument. She turned toward her mother for approval, but Mama's eyes had drifted shut, a pained expression on her face.

"Mama?" Serena said. "Mama!"

But Mama didn't respond.

Mama never woke up. After three excruciating days, she passed on to the next life.

Serena lived in a fog of grief until she determined that she would need to be strong for her father, who was heartbroken, and her sisters, who huddled together like orphaned chicks. She was glad they had each other.

The funeral took place with as much pomp as befitting a duchess of a grand estate. Although the attendance of ladies in the funeral procession, let alone the graveyard service, was forbidden, Serena begged her father to give her leave. To her surprise, Papa agreed.

"I've given you license for lesser things," he said. "Why would I deny you now?"

Serena kissed him on his cheek. "Thank you, Papa."

Everyone came from far and near, even Sebastian.

Their eyes met across Mama's burial ground. She expected him to still be angry at her for his dismissal, but his eyes only softened with concern. After everyone had paid their respects, he finally came up to her.

"I'm surprised to see you here," he said.

"I know. I begged Papa."

"You have him wrapped around your finger." He smiled.

She attempted a smile, too, but failed. She thought of Quinn's influence on Papa and mourned Sebastian's dismissal once again.

"I wish I could take your pain away, my lady," he said, his voice low. She gazed at him with admiration. He always thought of her comfort, above all else.

She wished she could run into his embrace and be held by him like she had when Crumpet went lame. She contented herself with his solicitous tone and loving glance. How she wished they could ride so she could forget her sorrows for the moment and confide in him.

Quinn was approaching them, however. Sebastian flicked a glance at him and bid her goodbye.

"What did he want?" Quinn asked, his expression darkening.

"He was simply paying his respects to Mama."

"That's all he'd better be doing." With that ominous warning, Quinn left her side.

Sebastian's boots trudged heavily through the icy slush building up along the pathway to the house. Nothing much had changed in the four years since he'd moved to Leitham Park, and now he was back for good.

The Bromley home was still the modest, two-story farmhouse he thought he'd outgrown. When he returned, his chest expanded with gladness at the sight of familiar things—smoke curling from the chimney, a sow and her young ones penned to the side, ice forming under the graceful bridge to the front entrance.

He had managed to stay away from Leitham Park, determined to forget Lady Serena.

Until Her Grace's funeral two weeks ago.

At the funeral, he was glad to get to speak to Serena, even for just a few stolen moments. Ever since, she resumed haunting his dreams.

The door flew open, and three children—two boys and a girl—came bounding out. "Sebastian!" Finn cried out. "Save me from these demons!"

He was the youngest of the boys, at six. Matthew was ten, as was Alice, his twin. His siblings had grown a lot since he had been home fully. Laughing, he caught Finn in his arms and tickled him.

"No, no, no," Finn said, wiggling out of his grasp.

Sebastian smiled, thankful there would be plenty of time to catch up before he journeyed to America. He entered the house and surveyed the domestic scene.

Three other siblings were helping in the kitchen—bookish Mary, animated Elise, and sunny Lucas. Mother eyed him warmly.

"Are you hungry?" she said.

His gurgling stomach confirmed her suspicions. He let his younger siblings lead him into the dining room, where a repast of pork pies and piccalilli awaited them. He ate the hearty pastry with the tangy condiment slowly. He noticed he was the only one eating.

"What's wrong?" he asked, looking around the table.

"You're leaving soon," Elise said, her smile faltering. She had gotten prettier over the years. She was almost eighteen, no doubt fighting off numerous suitors in the village.

Lucas reached for another pork pie. "Shouldn't that be a cause for celebration?"

Mary cast an exasperated glance at him. "You would be the first to cry your eyes out."

"I wouldn't," Lucas retorted. "Sebastian's taking me with him. Aren't you?"

Sebastian stared at his brother wordlessly. At some point, he had considered bringing a sibling or two. "One child leaving is enough of a heartache for Mother."

"Not if it's Lucas." Elise cocked her head cheekily.

Sebastian smiled through the banter until the conversation swirled without him. He sat there musing on his situation, of having lost his position in the duke's stables. Of having been cast out of the grounds where at least he could catch an occasional glimpse of Lady Serena.

He shook the image that came to mind—of Lady Serena in her scarlet riding coat, jumping the hedges on the hunt. An unparalleled equestrienne. A beautiful and courageous woman.

In the end, she had to choose her family and duty.

"What will you do now?" Lucas asked him, breaking his reverie.

"I will most likely try to find work at a different estate. I know they are always looking for fox hunt staff."

"The Glennis hunt is fast approaching," Mother said. "They expect it to draw a lot more folk this year."

Mary set down her cutlery and sipped her water. "If the roads aren't impassable this time of year."

"It's a lot colder this winter." Mother nodded. "That's certainly the case."

"When will Father come home for a visit?" Alice asked, her eyes wide.

"I would imagine soon," Sebastian said. "He was talking about coming in a fortnight."

There was a clamor at the door, and the three youngest children raced each other to open it.

"Is it Father?" someone asked.

"No, it isn't," Finn said.

Like the others, Sebastian gaped at their guest on the front porch. Lady Serena, in a thick, black winter cape, stood there with an apologetic glance.

Serena knew where everyone lived in the parish. She knew whose house this was. She'd hoped to avoid coming here, but the snow and ice made it necessary for her to plead for help.

"I am so sorry," she said, "but I'm afraid I am stranded."

After a surprised minute, Sebastian came to his feet. His shirt was loosened at the collar, and his shirt sleeves folded to his elbows. At the ducal estate, everyone was expected to dress formally. This was one of the few times she'd seen Sebastian dressed down, so to speak. And he was unnervingly attractive.

"Of course, come on in," he said. "Children, step out of the way now."

She entered. In her black mourning clothes, she felt like a crow amidst a roomful of color.

"Lady Serena," he asked in that low timbre of voice that left her flustered, "what brings you to these parts?"

She bit her lip. "I was going around to distribute donations, but the road is proving impassable. It's an icy bog out there."

"In a carriage?"

She shook her head.

Sebastian blinked. "You came on horseback? Without a groom?"

She could feel his censure, and the others' gazes on them. Back and forth. And his, intense and penetrating. "Yes. Luckily, I made my deliveries before . . . I no longer could."

"Of all the . . ." he muttered under his breath, causing her hackles to rise. Did he not think her capable of riding on her own? "Pardon me."

A middle-aged woman motioned for her to enter. "Well, then, no wonder this poor lass looks frozen. No need to be unpleasant, Sebastian." She smiled. Serena was looking at a feminine, more heavy-set version of Sebastian. "I'm his mum, Hetty."

"Pleased to meet you. I certainly don't want to impose." But Serena moved closer to the fire, happy to be out of the bitter cold.

"You aren't imposing. You've been so kind until—" Hetty fell silent, darting an uneasy glance at Sebastian. "That is—"

"It's all right," Serena said. "I apologize for the pain of your son's dismissal."

Sebastian stood off to the side, an expression of hurt crossing his handsome face.

"You've had your own sorrows," Hetty said. "I'm sorry about your blessed mother's demise, I am. It's hard to lose one's mother."

"Thank you so much for your kind words," Serena murmured.

"Draw nearer to the fire, my dear," Hetty said. "Thaw yourself out." She turned to Sebastian. "Why don't you take a minute, son, and take care of her horse?"

Serena turned. "I would be happy to come and help."

Sebastian was already on his way out, not looking at her. "Just stay here, Lady Serena. I'll make quick work of it."

With a sinking feeling, it was obvious to Serena that he was indifferent to her presence. Perhaps in the time they'd been apart, he was able to close his heart off as she should have closed hers. Serena hid her face and warmed it by the fire. She looked around once again and noticed the children watching her curiously.

She offered a smile. "You must all tell me your names."

When Sebastian entered, everyone was clustered around Serena. She sat on a bench near the fire enjoying a pork pie, the two youngest children tucked next to her. She raised her eyes to his, trying to look polite and unaffected by his return.

"I have sufficiently thawed out," Serena told Hetty, mostly for Sebastian's sake. "I appreciate your hospitality and will be going soon."

"Are you out of your mind, my lady?" Sebastian said.

Everyone, including Serena, gaped at him for the vehemence of his reaction.

"Sorry." Sebastian's gruff voice softened. "It's a proper blizzard out there. If you were to lose your way in it, you could die."

Serena looked out the window. The slush she'd ridden in had turned to huge flakes of snow. "I just worry that my family will not know my whereabouts."

"Why don't I send word out with one of our servants," Hetty said. "That way, your family need not worry themselves over your safety."

"That would be so kind of you," she said. "Hopefully, I will be able to leave tonight and not trouble you for too long."

Sebastian turned away, not affording Serena a glimpse of his expression.

Serena couldn't think of a lovelier evening in recent memory. Despite the humble circumstances of the Bromley home and Sebastian's bewildering annoyance with her, she was snugly warm and happy.

She gave up trying to remember everyone's names, though she took special liking to the youngest boy, Finn. He crept up to her a little at a time, giving her a funny glance now and then while he built up the courage to climb on her lap. The rest of the children were chatterboxes, and she soon learned what their passions and interests were. The older ones were beautiful and handsome in their own right.

Lucas looked like a younger and darker-haired Sebastian with a sunnier disposition. Mary was solemn and shy, but her blue eyes lit up when she favored Serena with her rare smile. Elise was more like Lucas, friendly and rather forthright, a stunning beauty, with her heart-shaped face and meltingly brown eyes fringed with thick, sooty lashes.

In all this commotion, Sebastian sat to the side nursing a hot drink while staring into the fire. Serena wondered how he was faring after being let go at Leitham Park. Seeing all his siblings possibly being dependent on him for their sustenance, she could imagine the burden and responsibility resting on his wide and capable shoulders.

Later in the night, the discussion turned to whether or not Serena could start heading home. But opening the door confirmed her fears that the weather had turned even more unpleasant, with heavy snow drifting across the landscape as to render everything undistinguishable.

"Elise, why don't you and Mary prepare your bedroom for our guest?" Hetty said.

Serena felt terrible on their behalf. They probably would have to squeeze in tight places with other siblings to make room for her. But she simply ducked her head, trying to not draw attention to the awkward situation.

Elise came up to Serena and touched the wool fabric of her gown. "Your clothes are beautiful."

"Thank you."

"May I look at the fine stitching?"

Over Elise's head, Sebastian's eyes met hers, his expression still somber.

"Of course," Serena said, motioning to her skirt.

Elise examined the material and expelled a deep sigh. "I would love to make a fine gown like this."

Serena stared at her. "A mourning gown?"

"The lines are classical, and the details lovely." Her eyes glowed. "May I sketch it?"

Serena sat for a sketching, acutely aware of Sebastian's glance flicking toward her once in a while.

As the fire started to die down in the grate, Hetty sent everyone away to get ready for bed. The children said good night to Serena with adorable little curtsies and headed to their respective rooms. As it happened, everyone but Sebastian left. The door was open, as was proper, but being alone with him made her heart race. She should have followed the older girls, but she felt compelled to stay to thank him.

She cleared her throat. "I cannot begin to thank you for your hospitality."

"It's nothing." Sebastian leaned close to the fireplace, scattering ashes with the poker.

"You could have turned me away. You were under no obligation to take me in."

"No," he said, turning a steady gaze her way. "No, we weren't. But of course, you shouldn't be surprised."

Her head spun. "I shouldn't? But I thought you were angry at me."

Surprise flit across his face. "Angry?"

"You've been annoyed and cold since I arrived."

He ran a hand through his hair, the disheveled locks over his brow adding to his attractiveness. "Because I was so afraid for your well-being. What if something had happened to you out there? What if you'd been hurt?"

"What then?" she whispered back.

He swallowed visibly, then spoke, low. "Then I should have been racked with grief."

His familiar speech shocked her, and yet . . . it felt natural and true as breathing. She gazed back at him without trying to hide her reciprocal feelings.

"I apologize," he said, sending a regretful look her way . . . tinged with hope.

"Don't. Please. It's nothing to feel sorry for."

His eyes locked with hers, and her blood turned to fire. He said her name in a strangled voice and took a step forward. Another. Until he was within arms-length. Serena sucked her breath in as he reached up with his hand and brushed a tendril off her cheek. His touch seemed to leave a trail of sparks.

His gaze scorched hers. "I would do everything in my power to protect you. You are always welcome in my home."

"Why?" she asked in a whisper.

"Do you really need to ask, Lady Serena?"

Serena couldn't breathe. Couldn't move. She felt a tug of desire as his gaze lowered to her mouth. The last few years, she had dreamed about Sebastian gazing at her this way. Being alone together away from the stables gave them leave to do so.

"Your bedroom is ready."

The couple sprang apart, Serena's head whipping to see an apology in Elise's eyes. "Pardon me for intruding."

"You weren't," Serena said in a hurry. She inclined her head vaguely toward the direction of Sebastian. "Good night."

"Good night," he said.

Someone had kindly laid out a nightgown on the bed in the small but tidy room. The garment was made of plain spun muslin, well-worn but soft and warm and embroidered with a pretty border. She wondered if Elise had made it.

She changed out of her dress and slipped the gown over her head, and then climbed under the covers, pleasantly surprised to find out that a bed warmer had already turned the sheets comfortable. Thinking of Sebastian's sweet sisters, she lay in the dark listening to sounds of the night and getting ready, a busy household with a lot of youth, and finally, a cozy silence.

She wondered where Sebastian slept.

What had he meant about doing everything in his power to protect her?

Would she wake up in the morning to that soft affection in his eyes?

Perhaps more importantly, should she encourage that show of affection?

Ten

Sebastian woke early to tend to the animals. Despite the still ongoing blizzard, he needed to get out of the house and clear his head.

Last night, he certainly lost all control. Before he could curb the impulse, he had come up to Serena, her beautiful eyes widening at his approach, and touched her hair. He would never have dared do that had they still been at Leitham Park. Everything at the estate reminded him starkly of the great divide between them.

Here at home, he could almost pretend they were equals.

Sebastian had shut his heart to the charming scene of her ladyship looking at home with his siblings.

Even he was forgetting himself. He was already starting to refer to Serena without her title.

He groaned with frustration over his lack of discipline. He had vowed to never show her his true feelings, as it was bound to only cause his heart to break.

"Something the matter?"

Sebastian nearly dropped the bucket of grains he'd been feeding the horses. He turned slowly, his chest tightening at the sight of Serena in her black cape and gown, elegant in contrast to the snow.

"You'll catch your death out here." He kept his voice gruff.

Her eyes danced. "Then why are you out here?"

He slanted his gaze at her. "I'm used to this, whereas you . . . aren't."

"Have you forgotten that I am a horsewoman," she said, arching an eyebrow, "and as such, I am well used to being out of doors?" She looked around. "The weather has not changed much since last night."

"You'll have to stay another day, perhaps." He kept his tone casual. Indifferent.

Tried to, anyway.

She sighed, flicking a playful glance at him. "Or two."

The minx.

He hoped for weeks-long blizzards.

He cleared his throat. "I have to travel today. I can bring a message to your family that you are safe."

"If it's too dangerous for me to travel, then you mustn't expose yourself to the elements."

He needed to run away, though. Have an excuse to not be around her. He could hardly contain his feelings. Especially as she walked right up to him and stood watching him grain the horses.

"How are you, Miss Crumpet?" she crooned to her horse.

Her gloved hand touched the gray horse's muzzle. Serena's skin showed between the gap from her glove and her arm, pale and smooth.

Sebastian averted his glance, busying himself by throwing in more grain.

"Sebastian . . ."

He turned, caught in her heady gaze.

"What are you going to do now that you are no longer in the employ of my family?"

He looked back at Crumpet, feeling dizzy at her nearness. "I've met with some landowners farther east. I hope to find work there."

"And then America?"

He nodded. "And then America."

"How much more money do you need before you can make that voyage?"

"At least five hundred more pounds for my passage and incidentals once I reach land."

"How about marriage?"

He cast a surprised glance at her. She was gazing at him from out of the corner of her eye.

His heart pounded unreasonably. "What about it?"

Pink spots burnished her cheeks. "Has a special miss caught your eye?"

He should lie through his teeth. She should never know.

But away from Leitham Park, he felt freer than he had felt all those past years. "Yes, for a long time now." He kept his eyes trained on Crumpet. "But I don't think she returns my affection."

She didn't say anything for a few seconds. "Are you sure of that?"

Sebastian watched Crumpet chew on her hay. "I can't possibly imagine that she would. She has her pick of all these beauxs."

"Perhaps," Serena said softly, "if you let her know how you feel, she would be emboldened, too."

He waited a few heartbeats, and turned to her. She had

cast her gaze down demurely, her lashes forming a thick fringe and hiding the expression in her eyes.

"Emboldened to do what?"

Her eyes flicked up at him. "To express her love for him."

What was she saying? His throat had constricted, and his mouth felt dry.

Was she referring to themselves, thinly veiled?

And then he remembered his goal of going to America. While Lady Serena had her life here.

It was one thing to entertain the fantasy that she'd want to spend the rest of her life in poverty in the vicinity of her family's estate, but to go to America with him?

He had better squash any hopes and dreams, because none of them would come true.

"It wouldn't do for her to do so," he said gruffly. "We have no chance for happiness." He backed up and set the metal bucket on the ground, upside down so snow didn't fill it.

He snuck a glance at her face. Her expression had wilted. He steeled his heart against her.

"Go on in and stay inside," he said, "where it's warm."

She didn't move. A shadow flitted across her lovely face.

He straightened up. "Please, Lady Serena."

Tears filled her eyes before she whirled and marched back to the house like he said. He should be happy, shouldn't he, that he'd not encouraged her? Then why did he feel as empty as the metal bucket at his feet?

Serena entered the Bromleys' home, her steps heavy as lead, her heart breaking into pieces. She wished she could hide from the rest of the world while she licked her wounds. But the entire family was indoors, helping prepare the next meal. She'd never seen such chaos—and such well-being.

"Good morning," Elise greeted her with her usual sparkle.

Too bad Sebastian wasn't as hospitable.

"Good morning. May I help?" she offered.

Elise and Mary stared at her, surprised.

"I wouldn't dream of it," Hetty said. "It would be such an imposition."

"I would love to learn," she insisted.

Hetty hesitated and then broke out into a huge grin. "Oh, why not? Come on over, and you can learn some of my grandmother's culinary secrets."

And that was how Sebastian found them—cozy and chatty and happily making crumpets. They smelled so good.

Serena's mouth watered just thinking of thick homemade jam on the fragrant, spongy pastries.

"Breakfast will be served here shortly," Hetty told Sebastian. "Why don't you wash up?"

As he passed Serena, his glance locked on hers before she wrested it away. At least she knew now that he didn't think anything could come of their infatuation. She needed to move on and accept it.

Then why did her traitorous heart keep wanting him?

They gathered round the table for a hearty English breakfast—bangers, crumpets with fresh jam, baked beans, and blood pudding. Lucas regaled Serena with stories from their childhood. She enjoyed his flirtations, though she decided he was far too young for her.

"Don't believe anything he says," Sebastian said. "He likes to spin a good yarn."

"Could it be that you're scared I will spill all your secrets?" Lucas retorted.

Sebastian rolled his eyes. "So long as she knows you can tell a fictional tale."

Lucas leaned forward. "There was a time when we were little—Sebastian was probably three and I was one—and he got it in his thick head to see how long I could hold my breath underwater. I was one, mind you. Not able to swim very well. Needless to say, our father fished me out before I turned blue."

Sebastian gave him a flustered look. "You make me sound positively mercenary."

"Things haven't changed since." Lucas winked at Serena.

Sebastian glowered at his brother. Serena suppressed a smile. Was he jealous of Lucas?

She could only hope.

After breakfast, everyone cleared in that happy,

ramshackle way that amazingly enough seemed to achieve things in the house. The older children invited Serena to skate on the pond.

Sebastian cast a glance out the window, and Serena followed it to where the sun couldn't cut through the dismal gray and relentless snowfall. "Cold enough, is it?" he asked.

"It's been cold enough for the pond to ice over," Elise said. She turned to Serena. "You can borrow Mum's skates."

"Yes, you certainly can," Hetty said.

"Thank you. I'll take you up on it," Serena said, trying to be lighthearted. "And then leave for home afterward, seeing that it's clear."

Hetty nodded. "What a splendid idea."

"Are you skating?" Elise asked Sebastian.

After their earlier conversation, Serena was sure he would say no, but to her surprise, he said yes.

Elise was all smiles. "That's set, then."

The little children begged to be included, but Elise made the decision to keep this activity for the older ones. "Mum will need your help," she said, amidst their dramatic groans.

They trudged through the slush and skirted the mud to a little pond at the back of their farm. Despite the gloom of the clouds, the snowy pond sparkled in places. It was a beautiful little spot of heaven. Serena glanced around at the frosted trees surrounding them.

"Do you like it?" Sebastian had approached so that they were side by side at the bank.

As his coat brushed her arm, it tingled. "Yes, very much so. This is beautiful."

"Not as beautiful as Leitham Park, of course." He darted an embarrassed glance at her.

"No. But that is all rather staid and manicured. This," she

gestured to the landscape with the sweep of her arm, "is natural. I almost expect fairies to make their appearance here."

"As they've been known to do so."

She gaped at him. "Truly?"

"We are only limited by what we imagine." His eyes gleamed as he moved away. He looked more attractive when he was smiling or lighthearted. She liked this side of Sebastian.

Minutes later, Serena tested the frozen surface in her borrowed skates. A layer of water covered parts of the ice from slush that was pooling on top. Serena skated along the side and then farther away as her confidence grew.

Sebastian skated alongside her. He was graceful for a man who was not built for such a dainty sport. She smiled to herself.

"What's so amusing?" he asked.

"I was simply thinking how we're almost skating in synchronicity. Like a dance." She wrinkled her nose. "We've never danced together before."

"Not on the ground, anyway."

She sent him a questioning glance.

He circled her. "We've ridden horses together."

"Ah, yes. Even better." Their gazes held and skittered away.

She recalled the times when they'd moved as one on their horses, riding with abandon over the heathers. How wonderful and carefree those days were. How innocent their friendship was.

Her heart ached that she could no longer be that same carefree girl.

They skated in a circle while the girls and Lucas threw snowballs at each other. When quiet Mary nailed Lucas with a snowball, Sebastian chuckled. Distracted by the commotion that ensued, Serena caught her skate in a rut and stumbled, putting out a panicked hand.

Sebastian caught it, his hand curling over her gloved one warmly.

Serena sucked her breath in. For a moment, she imagined them to be in a ballroom, dancing a set. Sebastian's hand squeezed hers before he let go, drifting past and whispering in her ear, "Careful."

His breath tickled her cheek, sending a delicious thrill down her spine. He kept his distance once again, but she was acutely aware of him as their strides got into similar rhythms.

They skated for another hour until the cold started to beset them. Serena and Sebastian fell quiet as they all trudged home. Though she was chilled to the bone, she wished they could stay out a little bit longer. As the path narrowed, Serena shifted closer to the middle just as Sebastian did, too, their arms brushing against each other's.

She lifted her eyes to his, before lowering them and feeling her pink cheeks turn even redder. They approached the house in the midst of a worsening blizzard. The ladies held on tighter to their bonnets.

"I'm afraid you won't be going anywhere tonight," Lucas told Serena.

Was Serena imagining things, or did Lucas almost look gleeful? With a bright glance darting toward Sebastian and then Serena, the corners of Elise's mouth turned up. "That's too bad."

Serena stole a glance at Sebastian. He raised his eyes to hers at the same time, and they simultaneously stifled a smile.

It was too bad, indeed . . .

Once inside the house, without advance discussion, Serena and Sebastian deliberately moved to opposite sides of the kitchen. Serena walked over to the window, glad she could be indoors on such a miserably cold night. Especially since she felt quite warm, and happy, for no explicable reason.

Twelve

Sebastian was feeding the animals early the next day when the Delaval carriage with its ducal crest pulled up alongside the house.

"You there," the footman said, calling up to Sebastian. "Have you seen Lady Serena of Leitham Park?"

Sebastian toyed with the idea of throwing them off her scent so she could stay with him permanently. "She's here."

At that moment, Serena came out. "Has my family missed me, Drumsby?" She was smiling playfully.

"Your father will be pleased to see your safe return."

"Let me enjoy my morning repast, and then I will ride home alongside the carriage."

Sebastian's spirits plummeted. He hadn't realized how painful seeing Serena go would be. He clutched at something, anything, to keep her close.

"I will ride with you," he declared. "To make sure the path is safe."

He felt foolish. No doubt she knew the grounds like the back of her hand, but she didn't argue. Instead, she gave him a sidelong glance, her expression softening. "I would appreciate that."

Sebastian turned back to his chores, his heart feeling light.

At breakfast, the children expressed their dismay that Serena was leaving. Sebastian sat quietly to the side, in silent agreement.

"We could ride together sometime," Elise said, her enthusiasm infectious.

"That would be lovely," Serena said.

Sebastian knew Serena was just being polite. That would most likely never happen. She would go back to her world, and his family would stay in his.

The younger children didn't hide their sorrow. Sebastian was almost envious of them—at least they didn't have to pretend a happy emotion they didn't feel. He stood and helped clear from the meal, though Mother shooed him off and said they'd better head back so that Serena could be reunited with her family right away.

Serena smiled. "My sincere thanks for the warm accommodations."

Outside, their breaths formed little puffs of clouds in the frozen air. Sebastian put some distance between him and Serena, even riding ahead so he didn't have to be tempted to keep staring at her. Occasionally, he would look back and catch her eye. She didn't look away, and instead returned his gaze with a sweet smile.

He turned forward, his heart hammering. He was not welcome in her household as a stable boy. What more as a son-in-law? They were doomed to suffer broken hearts.

Serena called for him.

Sebastian circled and rode abreast of her.

"I enjoyed your family's hospitality," she said. "I have never met a more engaging slew of siblings."

"I'm pleased that you find all of their quirks entertaining."

"Of course." She eyed him with curiosity. "Why shouldn't I?"

"I suppose when one sees individuals on a daily basis, you think there isn't anything special about them."

"Your siblings are fascinating, each in their own right."

"Oh?" Sebastian flashed a look at her, intrigued.

"Lucas was born to entertain a crowd. He would do well as a merchant, or as a performer. Elise would make a wonderful companion. She converses well and is quite intelligent without being condescending."

Sebastian's hands tightened over his reins.

"Mary would make a fine governess—" She stared at him. "Whatever is the matter?"

"Everything." He hadn't meant for his voice to have a hard edge to it. "Could you not hear yourself, Lady Serena? My family does not belong to your class, nor will we ever be."

She clutched her reins tightly, upset over his fatalistic attitude. "But you once said you have prospects."

"Even if I were to come to wealth, which is not guaranteed, I will never have the privilege of asking for your hand."

"Is that what you would like to do?" she asked quietly.

He decided to lay bare his soul, whatever the consequences. "More than anything in the world."

She blushed. "I wish you would."

Did she just say . . .

He guided his horse to sidestep a tall bank of snow as he allowed himself to exult in her words with a tenuous happiness.

Keeping her voice low, which was prudent since the carriage was within hollering distance, Serena continued. "Since you are speaking freely, Sebastian, I have some things to say, too. I care more about the people I love rather than my social standing."

"You've seen how we live, Serena," he countered. "It is not like anything you are used to."

"It's not, you are right. However, your home is full of love and laughter. Siblings who care for one another, and your mother is a good lady. I hold your father in high esteem."

"You will not be saying that when you have to endure privations." Sebastian made an impatient sound. "At the outset, our home will be modest, if not small. We will have to economize over clothes and food, and you will not be able to hire servants."

She bristled. "You have pointed out the bad. But there is also much good."

His shoulders sagged. "I am simply being realistic. I will be a tradesman who, right now, has no prospects. I have no money, no name, nor do I have any connections."

They had reached the edge of the forest past the hills that surrounded the stately Delaval mansion. Through bare branches, he saw the lines of the grand house, magnificent in the fog.

Soon, he would have to leave her there.

He may never see her again, and panic clutched at him.

With a lump in his throat, he watched Serena ride up to the carriage with nary a goodbye.

But she simply told the driver, "Go on ahead. I will take Crumpet to the barn and be inside shortly. Please have a groom meet me." The carriage went on rumbling down the path without them.

She wheeled her horse around and returned to his side. He tried to disguise his longing as they sat on their horses without speaking.

"Do you, or do you not, Sebastian Bromley, love me?" she asked, her brow arching.

Her boldness broadsided him. He was tempted to lie. His answer would determine the trajectory of her future. If he said no, he could let her go forever, to live the life she'd been bred to, with a titled or rich husband that her family would approve of. If he said yes, she would feel obligated to make an impossible relationship work.

He searched her eyes for clues. Her obvious affection tugged at his heart, imparting a calmness that he leaned on for strength.

"I love you," he admitted, in an almost wondrous whisper. "I have always loved you. You with your wild horse obsession." He smiled at the memory, and her lips trembled. "I've never met my equal since. In passion or zest for horses and riding. But most importantly, I saw into your heart. You are the kindest, most beautiful angel . . ."

"I haven't been an angel," she protested. "At any rate, I haven't been brave. Else, I would have fought for you. For our love."

Our love.

He let the delicious sound of that phrase wash over him. "Does that mean you love me as well?"

Tears filled Serena's eyes. "I love you. Everyone else pales against you."

"Even Lord Winthrop?"

Her lips twitched. "*Especially* him." Her smile wobbled. "I wish . . . I wish you and I could be together." She glanced at her gloved hands and back at him. "I am not sure if I ought to be glad for the blizzard. It gave me a taste of what I can't have."

He reached over and held her hand. "I'm no prince in a beautifully cut coat, with silk cravats. I am only Sebastian Bromley. I do not have wealth nor position—"

"I told you already," she said in a low voice, "I care nothing for those things."

He leaned forward and touched his forehead to hers. He could smell her sweet perfume and the scent of heather in the air. He leaned away and, with his thumb, traced her lower lip. She looked at him in a daze.

Leaning, he paused.

When she leaned toward him, too, he captured her mouth in his, the chill of the morn forgotten. He had long awaited this moment, this token of their love, and their first kiss was even sweeter than he imagined.

Serena was softness of snow and the beauty of winter. Her kiss held the promise of a safe and sure journey home. This was where they belonged—in each other's arms.

He kissed her once more. "When will I see you again?"

The side of her lovely mouth hitched up in a smile. "I want to see you every day."

"As much as I would like to do that, I am afraid to do so, I would need to address your father soon." Though he worried, her love for him gave him confidence.

"My dowry will be enough for us to take that voyage to America." She clutched at his hand. "I will pray that Papa gives us his blessing . . ."

Sebastian couldn't picture this happening. "Come away with me. We shall get married, and then we will go to America."

"But then my dowry would be forfeit."

"I know." He pressed a fervent kiss on her hand. "We'll

manage, you'll see." He let her go reluctantly, only to freeze up. In his line of vision past her shoulder, Lord Quinn, his eyes dark and furious, sat astride a majestic sorrel.

Thirteen

After taking Crumpet to the barn under the baleful glare of her brother, Serena and Quinn went to the drawing room, where Papa awaited them. Serena sat demurely on the settee, even as her nerves frayed. She clasped her hands on her lap, enduring the scrutiny of her father and brother. Quinn hadn't spoken this whole time, but watched the proceedings with interest—and, Serena thought, malice.

"I am most disappointed in you, Serena," Papa began. "I would have thought you have more sense than a flighty debutante. Are you so bent on bringing ruin upon our family's name?"

"I expected you to be disappointed, Papa, but would you have me deny the blessing of love in my life?"

"Love!" Papa roared. "No doubt this fellow found it so easy in his heart to love you, a duke's daughter with a sizable dowry."

"He loves me for me, Papa."

Papa turned away, shaking his head. "Although you are beautiful, my dear—a diamond of the first water as your mother was—there have been many bucks hoping to marry into our money. I have been careful to bring you up in the right circles, but apparently, I have not been careful enough. If only your mother's good sense prevailed."

At the mention of Mama, Serena turned her face to hide her sadness.

Papa paced and then stopped, glowering at Serena. "How do we take care of this . . . entanglement?"

Serena closed her eyes, weary at his interrogation. When she opened them again, Papa was looking at Quinn. "What do you recommend, son?"

"I think this man pursued Serena to spite you, Papa. I wouldn't give him the time of day, if I were you."

Serena sat ramrod straight. "That is not true! Sebastian has never spoken ill of any of you, though he may very well be justified.

Quinn lifted his chin. "He has turned you against us, that's what."

Serena turned her head, wanting to shut out Quinn's taunting.

"Papa," Quinn said, "may I talk to you privately?"

She willed Papa to stand up to Quinn and his overbearing ways. But Papa dismissed her. "I will call for you again."

Serena went up to her bedroom, throwing herself onto the bed. She rolled over so her back was on the coverlet and stared at the ceiling, painted with delicate floral blooms. Her gaze traveled next to the tapestries along the wall, framing the French windows.

She would be willing to give this up and more, if it meant that she could be with the man she loved.

Mama, her heart cried out. *I wish you were still alive.*

Surely, she would have stood in Serena's corner and advocated for her happiness.

When she heard the knock, she raced with eagerness to the door and answered it. "His Grace has called for you," the maid said.

Serena walked with troubled heart from her bedroom. Passing the portraits of her illustrious ancestors, she wondered what kind of story her portrait would elicit someday. Would hers be scorned for a loveless marriage or hailed for her bravery?

No one smiled at her return. Not Papa. Not Quinn.

"I have come to a decision," Papa said.

Serena sat on a settee and waited.

"If you choose to marry this man, I will cut you off. You may not use our title, nor refer to your pedigree . . . "

Serena turned hot and cold, trembling at the prospect of never being with the family. "Papa!"

He continued undeterred. "You will not get a dowry. Perhaps that will prove once and for all if this young man indeed loves you for you instead of your money."

Serena's eyes burned with unshed tears. She and Sebastian needed her dowry to survive. If she didn't bring that amount into their marriage, he would not be able to help his family. He would not be able to go to America. His dreams would die even before they could take flight.

"Papa." She leaned forward. "Won't you reconsider?"

His expression remained impassive. Did he no longer love her? "I have, and I must put my foot down sometime. You can stay with the family so long as you cut ties with this man. If you choose to marry him, you will be dead to me."

"But why?"

"Truthfully? I am trying to cure you of your disobedience. I don't want your sisters taking after your example without any thought as to the consequence."

"But Father, what about our family? I would want you to know my children—"

"Then choose wisely."

Serena shed tears on her way back to her bedroom. After her maid got her ready for the night, Serena excused her. She didn't want the maid to continue to be privy to her heartache.

If she chose Sebastian, she would go to him penniless, and her family would shun her. His dreams of going to America would be scuttled because he would need to spend the money he'd saved for his fare on their sustenance as a newly married couple.

If she chose to stay away from Sebastian, he would be able to take his voyage to America and reach his dreams. Without her as an added burden to him.

The dilemma filled her with sorrow. Either way, someone would be unhappy.

Fourteen

Sebastian waited for Serena, as they'd arranged, at the edge of Leitham Park's gardens. It had been a week since he last saw her. He missed her terribly and had come here as quickly as he could upon receiving her message.

Under him, his black gelding Simon could sense his nervousness and started to prance. Sebastian deliberately calmed himself. If she had bad news for him, she would have given him an indication, wouldn't she?

At every rustle in the wintry brush, Sebastian was sure Serena had arrived, but it was all just a false alarm.

Finally, the sound of hooves made him sit up and crane his neck. There was Serena, sedately walking Crumpet his direction. She cut an elegant figure in her black riding habit. His gaze followed her progress with delicious anticipation.

He smiled his welcome, but she only cocked her head in a reserved manner. His unease sent a panicked sensation down his spine. Why was she not smiling? Why had she stayed away so long?

"Serena." He said her name like a prayer.

She flashed him an awkward smile, filling him with apprehension.

Over her habit, she'd wrapped a fox stole. She pulled it close around her neck and shoulders. With the sun out, it was not uncomfortably chilly. Her movement spoke more of nerves than actually being cold.

She inclined her head. "Thank you for meeting me here."

"Of course."

"Shall we get off and walk?"

Sebastian dismounted and helped Serena down, keeping his hands on her waist perhaps a fraction of a second longer than he should have. He would have wanted to steal a kiss, but she averted her face. Sebastian knew now that something was, indeed, very wrong, but he continued on as though everything was as it should be.

"How is your family?" she asked.

"Very well, thank you."

"Did Elise start on the dress?"

"The dress?" He frowned. "I believe so."

"And Lucas, how is he?"

"Loud as always." He paused. "Will you come see them soon?"

"I'm afraid not."

She paused beneath the bower of an ancient tree as though tired out. He could already sense her withdrawing, but his heart continued to fight for their love.

"I can't be with you, Sebastian," she said.

The declaration echoed in the hollows of his heart.

She had given him hope, and now she had cut him down, adrift into an abyss. He had always known this in his heart of hearts, but her words were a death knell.

He closed his eyes to the pain, and then opened them again. She looked stricken with guilt.

"Why the change?" he wanted to know.

She watched geese fly overhead, their honking fading into the sky. "You were right. I thought more about what I would be giving up, and I couldn't. I just couldn't do it." She looked away.

His eyes narrowed. This did not sound like his beloved at all. Could she be lying? But why? He grasped her arm, forcing her to look at him. "I don't believe you."

Her gaze met his, and for a moment, she confirmed his suspicions. In the depth of her eyes, he saw love and concern. Had she truly changed so that the comforts of her family's fortune mattered more to her than their love?

A curtain seemed to fall in front of her face, obscuring the gentleness of her features. A glint of spirit flashed in her eyes. "Do you think so highly of yourself that you believe I would give up having the world at my feet for a lowly life with a stable boy?"

Certainly, she was joking. This was not the girl he had fallen in love with. He let her go. "Why do you persist with the cutting words?"

Her gaze dropped. "They're only cutting if they are true."

"So all your previous declarations, I suppose, *my lady*, were lies?"

Her voice sounded firm. "I may have felt those emotions at some point. I wish I could still say that I do. Perhaps being away from you cured me of my ill-judged feelings."

"Your ill-judged feelings!"

She made an impatient sound. "Do you intend to echo my every word?"

"And what of the kisses?"

She raised her eyes to his, then to his mouth. And then away. "What of them?"

He wanted to hurt her just as much as she was hurting him. "Did they not mean anything to you?"

She shook her head. "Perhaps not in the same way they did to you."

He didn't think it was possible to feel even more aggrieved by her coldness.

"And your warmth to me in that wretched little room in my family's house . . . that was all a sham?"

She raised her chin. "I was carried away in the moment, as I'm sure you were."

Angry hurt overcame him. He had given his heart to her, and here she was telling him she had fooled him. Without thinking, he grabbed her arm, causing her to lose her balance and stumble toward him.

He had not meant to kiss her. But now, smelling her heady perfume and having her standing so close, he could not stay away. His mouth covered hers.

He meant for this to be a punishing kiss. Without love. Just to teach her a lesson for playing fast and loose with his heart. For a moment, she struggled against his relentless grip. He loosened it now and pulled away from her. Shock registered in her eyes.

Remorse filled his chest. "I loved you then," he admitted, softly. "And I'll love you still."

This time, he kissed her gently as baby's breath. Delicate and sweet. He poured into that kiss his longing, his dashed hopes and dreams. He had wanted so much for them, but now, all that was gone.

After the kiss, he searched her eyes. Despite her remonstrances, he could tell he continued to affect her deeply. Her tortured gaze skittered away, soothing his pride and heart.

She took a step back and clasped her hands together. "I

must return to the house. I only came here to say goodbye. I . . . I wish you well on your journey to America."

The wind sliced through his thin coat. All his life, he had never been able to afford a thick one.

As his wife, she would not have the luxury of fox stoles.

She would be better off without him. This was the right thing to do. And yet his heart clamored for a chance.

But he wasn't so foolhardy as to beg for her love. A cold calm took over his heart, which he willed to silence.

"I wish you well in your life, Lady Serena." Without waiting for her reply, he marched back to his horse, mounted, and wheeled him the way he'd come.

Once the sound of horse hooves faded, Serena doubled over as though in physical pain. She was never one to lie. Oh, yes, perhaps she did over some of her more juvenile pranks as a young girl. But not about matters of the heart.

She had to, today.

She recalled Sebastian's face. The pain she'd caused him with this lie filled her with shame, but it was necessary. Had she hedged, opening the possibility that she still loved him, he might have insisted on pursuing marriage. But she couldn't let him.

She loved him so much that she was willing to let him go.

Allowing herself a good cry, she eventually straightened up and approached her horse. Against the cold of the winter chill, Crumpet's neck was warm, lending her strength to go on.

She took a deep breath, mounted, and headed back home to her family.

Fifteen

Serena spent the next several days in a stupor of pain, her heart aching with sadness. Her family acted as though nothing was amiss. As if she was invisible. Occasionally, Papa sent a concerned gaze her way, but his directive stayed in place. He never inquired after her, and there was never a chance for a private conversation.

Eventually, Quinn disappeared yet again on one of his usual pastimes. Serena was glad. She would never be able to forgive him for dismissing Sebastian out of turn, and for poisoning Papa against him.

Even the prospect of the fox hunt at Glennis didn't lift her spirits. She simply wanted to stay home. Papa, however, dangled a carrot.

"I have a green horse, Marmalade, who could benefit from an experienced hunter. Would you like to ride her?"

"Papa, I am tempted, but frankly, I do not wish be out in Society."

For a moment, Papa almost looked sympathetic. A

moment later, his expression turned stern. "Very well, your brother will ride her."

"Is this the golden palomino?" she asked. "She has too delicate of a carriage for a big man like him."

"So . . . will you help me out?"

"You have others in your employ who could help you, could they not?"

Papa lowered his voice. "I wish it to be like old times, my dear, when you and I were of one purpose, and able to ride out the dips and valleys of life."

Serena took in her father's appearance. His lip trembled, and his lined face looked haggard. With clarity, she realized that the past weeks since Mama's demise had been all too hard on him. She could set aside her concerns for a day and perform this kindness for her father.

"All right, I'll do it."

"Splendid." His expression softened. "I will admit that I like the company. No one but you seems to be able to keep up with me."

She paused then, an unspoken question dying to leave her lips. "Papa, I need your honest answer. Were it not for Quinn's objections, would you have allowed my match with Sebastian Bromley?"

He winced. "You are not being fair, my dear. Of course, what my firstborn says matters. I cannot simply ignore him."

"I cannot help but feel that had Mother still been alive, she would have given me her blessing."

"Enough." Papa's coldness cut to the quick. "Your mother is no longer with us. She was sheltered from the vagaries of life and would not have been aware of the privations you'd have been subjected to, had you defied me."

She stood. "Yours was a love match, and yet you deprive me of that same opportunity for love!"

Papa drew himself straighter. "I already said, enough. I thought you'd made your choice."

Serena fled to her room, her heart breaking because she realized she'd chosen wrong.

Sixteen

The Glennis fox hunt dawned frigid. Like Sebastian's heart.

He had stayed in the village next to the estate, keeping mostly to himself. Gentlemen spoke all around him about the impending day. The conversation at the tavern revolved around the quality of the hunters, the challenge of the course, and the caliber of the riders.

"I heard that the Duke of Delaval is coming, too. With his daughter."

Upon hearing this gossip from the next table over, Sebastian's heart clenched with pain.

With foreboding of a difficult situation, he returned to his lodgings and dressed with listless movements. He had not counted on seeing Serena any time before his voyage to America. He should have predicted they would join this fox hunt. Perhaps he should not have taken on this new post, though he did need the money.

He shook himself mentally. She had been so cold the last time. He could be equally cold. He determined that just because Serena was coming, it did not have to ruin his day nor his life.

Until he laid eyes on her once again.

He was talking to a fellow huntsman when she came into view, elegant and beautiful in her black riding habit. As though sensing he was watching, she turned, her surprised glance flicking right at him.

Despite the commotion of the hunt—the hounds, the people, the horses—it was as though they were the only people on that wintry valley. And despite his resolve, his heart still melted like a traitor.

He excused himself abruptly from the conversation and walked off to compose himself. With relief, he heard the gathering instructions from the hunt master. It was time to get ready.

This hunt attracted a larger crowd than Leitham Park's on Boxing Day. The weather cooperated nicely. Save for a short drizzle, it was largely dry. The terrain did not appear to be treacherous, but the hunt master warned about slippery conditions, nonetheless.

From Sebastian's vantage point, he could see Serena, surrounded as usual by a bevy of admirers. The sight would have rankled at him in the past, but today, he prided himself on being immune to hurt. She could very well flirt with whomever she pleased.

The hunt master blew on his horn, unleashing the hounds, followed by the horses and their riders. Sebastian exulted in the thrill of the ride and being able to have his horse stride out strong. Soon, he broke a little ways from the pack so that he could traverse the first few jumps.

Lady Serena was hard to ignore. Her elegance on a young palomino kept appearing in the periphery of his vision. His attempts at ignoring her failed dismally. As they spread out into a clearing, Sebastian pushed his horse into a gallop. Nearby, he could sense that Lady Serena matched him stride for stride.

Up ahead, he noticed a fallen tree trunk. He could see it clearly from his horse's perch, but in a split second, he wondered if Lady Serena did. Shrubbery obscured her path. If she did not clear it . . .

He called her name and the directive, "Log ahead!"

Her eyes widened as the words permeated her consciousness. In the next moment, she lifted Marmalade's head and sailed into a jump.

She did not clear all of the log in time. Sebastian heard a thwack as Marmalade's hoof clipped the wood. Horse and rider both disappeared on the other side. Only the horse came up in a prance.

Sebastian was not obligated to stop for her. He had been hired to help with the hunters. Others were charged with caring for the fallen riders. But he did not even think twice about circling around and sliding to a stop where Serena's still body lay.

Sebastian could hear someone dispatching the others around the obstacle and clearing the brush. He needed to move Serena where she would be safe. He carried her a few horse-lengths to the side, where anyone could better see them, and knelt over her. Whispering her name in a panic, he hoped against hope she could hear his voice.

Seventeen

When Serena did not respond, Sebastian pressed his finger against her slender throat and felt a thread of a pulse. At first, it throbbed weakly, then strengthened. A wave of relief broke over him.

"Serena," he said, "can you hear me?"

Her eyes fluttered open, unfocused. And then a spark of recognition flared. "Sebastian. You came for me."

Joy leaped in his breast. "Of course, I would come for you."

"You didn't need to. There's others to attend to me. But my horse—"

"Is safe. She's walking about."

Her expression calmed. "Good. Silly Marmalade."

"Can you sit up?"

"Perhaps?"

He raised her to a sitting position, all the while trying to ignore the palpitations her nearness wreaked in his chest.

She leaned against him, causing him much alarm. "Are you all right?"

"No," she said, her voice muffled against his coat. "I am definitely not all right."

"Would you like smelling salts?"

"That won't help my malady."

He touched her forehead with the back of his hand. "Are you feverish?"

"Undoubtedly."

She flicked a laughing glance at him, while still leaning in the circle of his embrace. He was sure she had hit her head, for she was looking at him tenderly.

"My dear Sebastian," she murmured. "I have been wrong. So terribly wrong."

At the sound of the endearment, Sebastian thought *he* had hit his head. He felt dizzy.

Her mouth trembled. "I have done you a grave harm. I told you I had no feelings for you, and that our kisses meant nothing." Her eyes glimmered with passion. "I *do* have feelings for you, and your kisses *do* mean something. *Everything.*"

By now, the crowded passel of horses had passed them by. One of the huntsmen slowed, but Sebastian waved him on. "Things are under control here!"

"That is a lie," Serena said with a wry smile. "My poor heart is doing all sorts of acrobatics."

"I don't understand," he said, still holding her tightly against him. "If you are simply being impulsive, I don't think I could stand another heartbreak."

"I've decided to come clean, that's what."

"Are you saying that you . . . love me?"

She nodded, pressing her cheek against the lapel of his coat.

He inhaled the sweet scent of her hair. "Then why did you deny it?"

Raising her eyes to his, she blinked. "Because I love you."

He shook his head. "That does not make any sense."

"I know. I am sorry." She paused. "My father threatened to cut me off if I were to marry you. I would be dead to him."

Sebastian's heart ached for Serena. To lose her family over him! "That's a steep price to pay. I can see why you changed your mind."

"No," she protested. "It's not that at all. You see, coming to you penniless, I would be a burden."

"Well, yes, but you needn't worry about the money—"

"But how would you fulfill your dream of going to America?"

"I have a sizeable savings."

She gave him a skeptical look. "But if we get married, we would need a home, and when children come—"

"Hush, my darling. We will be all right. I promise you that." Were they really talking about marriage? Was he dreaming?

Serena reached up and touched his cheek. She was flesh and blood. Not simply a figment of his imagination. "In turn, you must promise you will not give up your dream for me."

"Why do you worry about that so?" He stared at her, baffled.

Her eyes flashed. "I don't want you to tell me later how I prevented you from pursuing your dream."

He smiled and traced her cheek with his gloved finger. "What about you, Serena? What is *your* dream?"

"Are young ladies allowed to dream beyond securing a perfect marriage?" She glanced modestly at her hands. "I want a happy household, with enough for common comforts. I want to be the mother of children who will grow to be responsible adults and contribute to society." She returned her gaze to his. "And most of all, I want at least one horse who can take me places and accompany me when you are far from home. Can you give me that much, Mr. Bromley?"

"Consider it done," he promised. "But first, we must whisk you off somewhere more comfortable than this abominable bog, or risk having us smell of mud all day."

"So what's new?" Her smile faded as she touched his arm. "How shall I get away?"

His brow looked troubled. "I know my chances are grim. But I would like to still offer for you, my love."

"But that would be insanity!"

"It would be the honorable thing for me to do."

"And if he says no, as I believe he would?"

Sebastian pressed her gloved hand to his lips. "Give me a few days to make arrangements. We would have to take a carriage . . ."

Serena clung to him. "I'm afraid."

"You mustn't be. Either way, we will be together." With this promise, he kissed her temple.

Eighteen

Serena allowed Sebastian to carry her over the grasses and mud, settling her on the back of her mount. Why he fussed, she could not fathom, when her riding habit had already been ruined beyond hope, between her tumble and the soggy flora.

"I can always replace my habit," she said, laughing. When a shadow flitted across his face, she realized the folly of her words. No doubt he was calculating how much he would need to acquire for income to maintain a lady of rank, unused to privation.

"I do not wish to curtail your merriment today," he said, attempting a brave smile, "but those are the kinds of things you may not be able to do for a while— if at all—when you take my name in marriage."

Although she waved off his concerns, she fell into deep thought. She mulled his words as they rode back to the start of the hunt, for they had by then given up on the notion of catching up with the rest. Was it so very fair that she would be judged for the rest of her life based on what she was used to growing up instead of what she could become?

"What does your mother do to support your family?" she asked.

"She doesn't have any particular livelihood. She does economize on many things because we are such a large family. Over the years, she learned to make soap, and staples like cheese. All from the stock of our farm. I certainly don't expect you to work to bring in some income."

"But I want to. It is only right that I try to lighten your burden however I can. I was thinking that perhaps I could start a dress shop with your sister, Elise."

"A dress shop?"

"Why, yes. I have been around fine fashion all my life, so why shouldn't I parlay that knowledge into good use? And Elise has the drive and temperament to run such a venture."

His skeptical expression turned into admiration. "I didn't think you'd known them long enough to make such judgments, but you're correct. Elise has a good eye for clothing and art. I daresay she gives our mother an apoplexy for showing up in beautiful threads when she merely is clever enough. The appearance of expense worries her."

"I wouldn't be surprised if someday, she is to attract the eye of a gentleman. She is polished and poised, and a pleasure to be around." And then Serena remembered. "But we're leaving for America. I can still get her started."

Sebastian smiled. "With that in mind, tell me then what you perceive Mary's future will be."

"I believe I've said before—she could be governess to a family. I would refer her for my sisters were it not that my brother, I'm sure, would object—"

Frustration mounted within Sebastian. "He has no moral authority to lord over you."

Serena gave him a sad smile. "I have long given up hope that my brother will regard me with anything other than ill-will. I am a pesky female who stands between him and my father. Papa, in his grief, leans on him much more than before and will not hear reason." A tear spilled from her eye, and she brusquely wiped it off. "I wish Mama never died. She was always a reminder to Papa of everything beautiful."

Sebastian comforted her with a warm embrace, making Serena feel much better. The delicate matter of their possible marriage, of course, still needed to be broached.

"Perhaps Papa will have changed his mind," she said, half to herself, to buoy her spirits.

As the rest of the hunting party joined them, however, the Duke of Delaval made a direct cut to Sebastian, coldly ordering Serena to come along. She gave him an anxious parting glance, conveying her love through her eyes.

When they reached their home, Serena nervously waited in her room. An hour later, she heard the arrival of a horse and rider and ran downstairs. Standing in the grand vestibule, Sebastian raised his eyes to her with a loving expression and calm demeanor. How she admired his courage. The butler returned, asking Sebastian to follow him into the library. Serena consoled herself that by indicating the library, Papa at least placed him in a room with dignity, rather than, say, the stables.

Quinn entered the house, strolling by languidly. "I cannot possibly imagine why that most odious man has come here, do you?"

"He's been most respectful," she retorted.

"He most certainly is presumptuous, and I do not like how he does not defer to his superiors."

"You must mean superiors in birth," Serena could not resist saying, "because it certainly isn't superiors in intellect."

Quinn glared at her. Serena was saved from an aggrieved tongue-lashing when a servant asked for Serena to join her father in the library. Serena went down the hall, trying to appear composed, though she quaked with nerves.

Papa looked up. He was alone.

"You sent him away," she said faintly.

"Yes, I did. Through the back where he belongs."

Her poor, darling Sebastian.

Papa continued. "I didn't want him hanging about and trying to finagle an audience with you."

Serena was glad that Quinn was not in the room. He would have sped Papa's decision to turn down Sebastian's suit.

"That young man made two interesting propositions."

"Two?" Serena said faintly.

"The first, which shouldn't come as a surprise to anyone—though the massive impertinence rankles—was to ask for your hand in marriage."

"And you said?"

"I said over my dead body."

His pronouncement did not shock Serena, but her happiness faded. The die was cast. She would be saying goodbye to family. To her dear Papa.

"I said, furthermore," Papa's voice rose, "that if he so much as showed his face at my property, I would have him shot."

She gasped with alarm.

"Papa, you are most cruel! You said if I chose to marry him, I would give up this . . ." She gestured around. "Everything." She stood her ground. "I choose to marry him."

He stood, circled his desk, and leaned against it. To her surprise, she could see pain in his eyes. She looked away. She did not want him to weaken her resolve. She would marry Sebastian.

"I cannot allow you to make this mistake." As his words began to sink in, he said, "You will stay on this estate for as long as you insist upon this abominable alliance. When you are ready to exercise common sense, you may return to Society."

She blinked back affronted tears. "You mean I will be a prisoner in my own home!"

"This mansion is hardly a prison. Look around, my girl, and tell me that all these comforts induce suffering."

"Papa, I beg of you to let me marry Sebastian. If Mama were still alive—"

His mouth twisted. "If she were still alive, she would have prevailed upon you to turn your thoughts away from this opportunist."

"I do not believe she would. She would, perhaps, even threaten to leave you had she been witness to your perfidy!"

Serena quailed at the fury on her father's face.

"Begone!"

"I will if you will answer one more question," she said, remembering. "What was his second proposition?"

Papa sneered. "He offered to help me invest in some horses he's breeding."

Bewildered, she asked, "After you had declined his offer for my hand?"

"In addition to. He seemed to think that would sweeten the deal. He knows fully well there is nothing to commend him to me. Nothing."

Serena would have sat down then, for her energy flagged. Her father just eliminated her one true chance for happiness. Anything else that came after this would pale.

"Serena." His voice softened.

She gazed at him with wary eyes.

"I will let this little indiscretion slide. In fact, I take full blame for it, allowing you to run like a hoyden all over our estate in the company of stable hands. I should have known that would not bode well. No one need know about this. You can still attend the next Season and meet a fine young man who would be more suited for our class."

"You mean like the Earl of Winthrop?"

"Yes, I would favor that match."

Serena wanted to scream. All she could think of with a crust of bitterness was that Papa was going against his word. She would try one more time.

"Papa, you said I could choose to marry him and give up my ties with the family."

Papa's face turned red. "You foolish girl," he shouted, "out of my sight. You will do no such thing, and I will hear no more of it."

The dam broke then. Serena sobbed while Papa looked on, not doing anything to console her. She was not sure what broke her heart more—that she couldn't be with Sebastian, or that she could no longer count on her father for protection. After a few seconds that felt like a lifetime, she fled to her bedroom.

Nineteen

Sebastian waited by the copse of trees leading to the forest around Leitham Park. He had not been shocked by the duke's firm and almost violent refusal of his offer. When the duke asked the servants to take him out through the back like the day's garbage, he knew with a sinking feeling that that would be the end of the matter unless they eloped.

Elopement to Gretna Green could certainly be an option, although it pained him to subject his sweet Serena to such ridicule. But if that was the way to be with Serena, he would do it.

When he heard the hooves of a horse in hot pursuit, he raised his head in alarm. Perhaps the duke had sent an assassin to finish him off. He would not put it past him, as vehement as his opposition had been during their conversation. When the horse and rider came into view, however, Sebastian breathed a sigh of relief. He raised his hand to greet his father.

The elder Bromley frowned. "I know what happened," he said. "A servant generously shared with me the news. You put me in a fine position, lad."

"I am sorry, Father. That was not my intent."

"Then what was your purpose?"

"I merely wanted to offer for the woman I love. Since he refused, she will have the option to come away with me instead."

"You are delusional, Sebastian. I raised you to be smarter than that. She would be cut off from her family. Have you forgotten that I have known her as long as you have? I also want what is best for Lady Serena. It is not you."

"You, too, Father?" Sebastian sighed. "I thought perhaps I could count on you to understand."

His father's expression hardened. "Look at me, son. You know I am no sluggard. I labor as hard as the fellow next to me. I have worked in grand houses such as this one. When I was younger, I did not have good looks or income to catch every lady's eye, but I was a good horseman. As such, I was allowed into circles similar to yours—as a groom to a wealthy family . . . with beautiful daughters. I could have run off with one of them, had I allowed our misguided feelings to develop. But I did not. I searched for a maiden in our village, and that is how I came to pursue your mother. Now aren't you glad I made that choice?"

"Certainly," Sebastian said, brooking no argument. "I am grateful, for Mother is an angel to put up with a son like myself and all my siblings. But I have not a lady like her I'm pining for. Lady Serena and I have not taken this decision lightly. She is prepared for censure if only to assure our happiness. She understands that she will go through hardships and strife, and will lose one of the things she holds dear—her family."

Father grimaced. "Are you so selfish as to drive her to not just starvation of the stomach, but also of her spirit?"

"Father, I will not debate you on this matter anymore. I recognize the precariousness of your position. I will make myself scarce soon, but I beg of you that as I await word from her, you will allow me to stay here unmolested."

"I cannot guarantee anything." Father's face darkened with anger. "My loyalty is to my employer, not to my dunderhead of a son!"

Father turned his horse and galloped in the direction of the stables. Sebastian watched him with sorrow. If Serena joined them in their household, would his father welcome her? He knew Mother would, for she was the loving and forgiving sort.

After several minutes, Sebastian decided that Father's threat of turning him in was empty. No one came to accost him, even as the afternoon turned into night. As frost bit his skin, Sebastian decided to turn around and go home. He would return the next day . . . and the next. Whatever it took to be with his love.

Twenty

Serena's fingers pounded heavily over the keys of the pianoforte. The music—sad and melancholy—matched her mood, as did the rolling fog outside. Suddenly, her fingers crashed on the keys, punctuating the afternoon stillness with a discordant note.

"Must you make such a noise?" Quinn lamented. "Your Grace, I beg of you to silence your daughter."

He already has, the words rang out in Serena's head.

Serena stopped playing, not turning to look back at her father and her brother. The silence stretched into an oppressive quiet. She made a big show of shutting the cover to the musical instrument, until Quinn huffed once again. "For pity's sake! Serena, must you bang it shut?"

Again, Serena did not answer. What was there to say? If they were to keep her a prisoner in her own house, then by all means, she would not be pleasant.

"I'm going for a ride," she announced as she got to her feet.

"Sit down, Serena," Papa ordered. "You aren't going anywhere outside."

She turned to challenge him with her gaze. What would he do? Drag her by the hair to a chair and tie her up?

They did not stop her when she fled from the room. She heard some voices down the hall, in the girls' nursery, and poked her head in. They were playing with dolls, conversing animatedly.

Serena smiled even as her heart contracted with pain. If she were to marry Sebastian, she would never see her sisters again. She walked into the room, the governess and the girls looking up at her in surprise.

"Come girls," Serena said, trying to sound cheerful, "sit and I'll read you a book."

She picked an engaging storybook about a cat who journeyed to the king's palace. When she was done, she hugged her young sisters and kissed the top of their heads.

"Are you crying?" Margaret said.

Serena shook her head. " You girls be good." Then she walked purposefully down one set of stairs and another until she was running and breathless. At the door, a footman barred her way.

"Let me pass at once," she said in her most authoritative voice.

"Pardon me, my lady, but your father gave express orders—"

So that was why her father did not worry. With a moue of disgust, she turned at the heel and walked off to a window, where she watched the arrival of a carriage with interest.

It was, miracle of miracles, her dear friend Amelie in her family's carriage.

Serena ran to the door, where the footman stood. "Let me

pass. I have a visitor."

The footman looked uncertain. Serena made an impatient sound and ducked under his arm, running to meet Amelie.

"You cannot guess how *happy* I am to see you," she greeted her friend.

Amelie laughed at Serena's enthusiasm. "It is a pleasure to see you, too. I would have ridden over, but the weather has been abominably cold—"

Her friend would have stepped out of the carriage, but Serena blocked her way. "Let's go for a carriage ride, Amelie."

Amelie looked dubiously at the cloudy sky. Rain began to fall in earnest, hardly making for a day of going about. "Are you sure?"

Serena winced. "I couldn't be surer of anything in my life." And with that, she jumped in next to her friend.

In the carriage, Amelie listened with a furrowed brow to Serena's story. "I cannot imagine the duke acting in such a cruel manner," she cried. "My heart breaks for you."

Sorrow threatened to drown Serena. "Between Mama's passing and Quinn's increasing influence, he has not been himself."

"Serena, please do not take this wrong, but could it be that they are simply watching for your own good?"

"Alas, I wish that were the case. Like I said, Quinn is watching for his own good."

Amelie patted her arm. "You must love this man so much to give up your home and family."

Serena gave her a tremulous smile. "Yes. Yes, I do."

"Sebastian Bromley had better be worth all this." Amelie winked. She leaned forward and clasped Serena's hands. "Tell me, my dearest friend. What can I do to help?"

Serena studied her friend's heart-shaped face, framed by her pretty hat. Such a beautiful creature, inside and out. How blessed she was to have such a loyal friend.

Twenty-one

Sebastian's heart raced at the sight of a carriage arriving posthaste at his doorstep. Could the duke have sent some runners to take care of him? When the door flew open, revealing his beloved, he gasped with relief and ran outside as fast as he could.

Serena ran into his open arms, enveloped in his loving embrace. He stroked her hair and kissed the top of her head. She raised her puckered lips, and he laughed shakily. He kissed her, to his family's various stages of wonder and amusement.

Serena's friend waved from the carriage.

"Amelie is my guardian angel, darling," Serena said. "She happened to come to my door, so I escaped. Papa wouldn't let me out of the house."

Sebastian turned grateful eyes to Amelie. "Thank you."

"We haven't a lot of time." Serena tugged at Sebastian's sleeve. "Someone has surely given a hue and cry by now. Let us go."

He blinked in confusion. "Go where?"

"Why, to Gretna Green." Her smile dimmed. "Unless you changed your mind?"

"No, I haven't." He touched her cheek. "I just wish I could give you a proper wedding. And everything else!"

"I know you do." She leaned into his embrace. "After the wedding, we can worry about other things." Her eyes widened. "Speaking of which, I haven't a single thing with me."

"You can buy what you need along the way," Amelie suggested.

"I considered taking out a special license," Sebastian mused. "But no, your father is an influential man. I would not doubt that he would catch whiff and put a stop to it at once. Already, I have been shunned by horse breeders after Lord Quinn dropped unflattering comments about my work ethic, or lack of it."

Serena looked pained. "I wish I were of age!"

"Poor child," Mother called from the house. "How about if we give you some hot soup?"

"Thank you, Mrs. Bromley," Serena said, "but we're off to be married."

"Heavens," Mother said, putting a hand to her throat. "You don't say."

Mother sidled over to Sebastian. "Son, what are you doing? This lady deserves far better treatment than what you are giving her."

"Which is what I'm doing. Her father imprisoned her against her will. Surely, that was no better than this."

Mother tut-tutted. "Fathers are supposed to protect their daughters."

He could see Serena's head averted as though she were trying hard to not listen. They should not keep secrets between them. He walked over to Serena and put an arm protectively around shoulder.

"Precisely," he said. "And when they are derelict in their duties of fairness and decency, then a child must manifest her own destiny." He smiled at his mother. "We will need to be on the road soon. We'll send word when we've settled somewhat."

"Fare thee well, young lovers," Mother said.

"When you return," Elise told Serena with twinkling eyes, "I will have made you a gown or two."

"I look forward to seeing it," Serena said. They beamed at each other, already like true sisters. Hugging Amelie tightly, Serena got in her friend's family carriage, followed by Sebastian.

Twenty-two

Four days later, near Gretna Green, Scotland

The carriage lurched, waking Serena. They had been traveling by Amelie's carriage now for four days. They had stopped several times along the way for a fresh change of horses and night accommodations, attracting censorious glances from strangers who no doubt speculated someone was running off to Gretna Green.

Their opinion did not matter to Serena. She loved Sebastian, and he loved her. Soon, they would be able to wed, and her father would no longer be able to object or derail their future.

Sebastian was awake and gave her a sweet smile that tugged at her heart. As they crossed the river into Scotland, Sebastian reached over and covered Serena's hand. She basked in the warmth of his touch. Against the dark purple—nearly black—of the new gown they had purchased along the way, her skin looked pale.

"You're cold," he observed. "Are you afraid, my darling?"

"A little," she admitted. "Until we are married, I feel like something else might happen to prevent us from being together."

"Such as?"

"Oh, my father showing up . . ."

"Or wild horses running."

"What?"

"Wild horses won't stop me from marrying you." He gave her a lopsided smile, and his hazel eyes twinkled. His light tone lifted her spirits.

"They'd better not. We'll have to catch them and add them to our barn."

He leaned over, and meant to only plant a light kiss on her lips, but the carriage lurched once again, throwing her into his arms. When the carriage stopped in earnest, they pulled apart from the most delicious kiss.

"We're here," Sebastian said unnecessarily, both of them smiling at each other.

He helped Serena out of the carriage. Serena blinked against the morning light. Or perhaps his nearness dazzled her. At any rate, the bright sunshine was a harbinger of good things.

They made their way to the first blacksmith shop where they could be wed as husband and wife. Serena looked down at her dusty hem. Her hair had started to come undone.

She had always dreamed of a lovely wedding in a church, but she tamped down that girlish dream. She loved Sebastian, and that was all that mattered . . .

"Would you like to freshen up before our wedding?" Sebastian regarded her with tender concern.

His sweet gesture was all it took for her to feel calm once again. She nodded, and they stopped at an inn to inquire after a washroom. Serena was grateful for the quiet moment. In just a few minutes, she would be married to her love. Even though she was doing the right thing, it was a big step.

She dried her hands on a towel and came out, gasping. For standing just outside the washroom was Papa.

Twenty-three

"How did you find me?" Serena said, her throat tightening.

"I saw Amelie's carriage, and so I guessed you might be here. Serena." Exhaustion was plainly written on Papa's face. "I have chased after you all these days. Come home with me, now."

A calm took over her. She was no longer afraid of what her father could do to her. "You will have to drag me kicking and screaming, Papa."

"Really." He stared her down. "Is this how you would treat your father?"

"I thought I respected you, Papa, but since you started doing Quinn's bidding, I no longer hold you in such high esteem."

Papa studied her face. "I must ask you for one more chance. A test, if you will."

She gazed at him as though he was playing a trick. "Tell me, and we'll see."

"I want you to see for yourself how your supposed

beloved acts when he thinks you are not observing him. There is a curtain in this receiving room. Hide yourself and listen in on our conversation."

"Are you trying to trick him, Papa?"

"I am merely trying to expose his character. If, indeed, he has one."

She glanced at him skeptically, not wanting to subject Sebastian to any ridicule. "You will lose this bet, Father, so you may as well say goodbye to me now."

Papa's features sagged with sadness.

"Goodbye, Papa," she said. She did not think her heart could break further, but it did. Then, as he asked, she stepped behind the curtain and waited.

The door to the hostelry opened, accompanied by the sound of boots.

Sebastian growled, "If you have done something with my intended . . ."

"I haven't. Keep your voice down." Papa paused. "I am making one last offer. An offer I believe you will not be able to refuse."

"Nothing you say will sway me from marrying your daughter. You might as well spare me your insults."

Papa sighed audibly. "Young man, I have five different studs from the Godolphin lines, whom I have, up till now, limited access to the stables of only very close friends and associates. Their sires will fetch a handsome sum, enough to make you a man wealthy beyond your dreams. And if you breed them—"

"I know their value," Sebastian growled.

Serena did, too. Sebastian would be insane to turn down such an offer.

But what of their love?

Papa continued. "If you leave my daughter alone, I will recommend you to a good stable. Otherwise, you can rest assured that I will blacken your name high and wide. You will never be able to work in horse breeding for any grand house ever again. Picture yourself, in the poor house, with my willful daughter. Soon, she shall break and snap—"

"Listen here, Your Grace." Sebastian's voice lowered. "Thank you for the generous offer. I am not delusional enough to not recognize the enormity of what those horses could do for me and my livelihood. I have always admired your stock, and I know their value."

Serena held her breath. If he said yes to that, she could not blame him. Even just a single horse from her father's barn was sure to fetch a handsome stud fee.

"However . . . nothing you could give me can ever stop me from loving your daughter. Yes, I love her. I want to be with her the rest of our lives." Strong emotion threaded through Sebastian's voice. "You can keep your horses, your money, your connections, and your jobs. I will give up *everything* for your daughter."

There was a long stretch of silence. Serena's heart bit back tears, moved as she was by his speech and his passionate declaration.

Finally, Papa spoke. "Very impressive, Sebastian Bromley, even if I think you're still an opportunistic stable boy."

Serena trembled and closed her eyes. Would Papa never let up? But then he said, "From this day on, my daughter is dead to me. And I do not want to see you nor your family ever again."

Papa, came Serena's silent, anguished cry.

This bit brought tears to Serena's eyes. It was quiet save

for the ticking of a clock somewhere. There was the sound of a door opening and closing, and a deep, deep sigh from a heroic man.

Her husband to be.

Her heart leaped at the thought.

She peeked out from her hiding place. Sebastian was standing by the window with his hands in his pockets, staring out into the Scottish morning. At her approach, he turned, his eyes warming with pleasure.

"I heard what you told my father," she confessed.

He blinked. "You did?"

She nodded. "You turned down perhaps the best thing that could have been offered to a horse breeder. It could have meant an amazingly lucrative stable."

He held out his hands. She came to him eagerly.

"No, my darling," he said, "*you* are the best thing that could ever have happened to me."

With a little happy sob, Serena melted into his arms and was soon lost in the haze of a wondrous kiss. With some reluctance, Sebastian pulled away.

His eyes gleamed with happiness as he offered his arm. "Shall we get married, my love?"

Epilogue

Twenty years later, Fenshire Castle, England, 1820

From the carriage, Gabrielle Bromley watched the English countryside pass in a lovely blur.

Sad that it had taken her nineteen years—her lifetime—to finally reach the shores of England. Mama seldom talked about her birth country, but when she did, Gabrielle pictured exactly this—everything unbelievably lush and green, fog rolling across the hills, and wide open spaces that they lacked where she had lived in New York.

In her portmanteau, she had tucked the letter her mother had received from her girlhood friend, Amelie, and she took it out now.

Dearest Serena,

I received your letter with pleasure. How wonderful that your daughter has taken after you in her love of horses. Yes, I still ride and have children who appreciate our wonderful four-legged friends—in various sorts of ways, not necessarily riding all day like we did when we were young girls.

As for your inquiry about a potential household where your daughter could be employed as a companion, coincidentally, we have been wanting to secure such an individual for our daughter, Daphne. Would Gabrielle be interested in joining our household? If so, please let me know so I can send a little token to help with her passage from America.

The rest of the letter blurred in her grateful tears. To her mother. To her mother's friend.

The carriage slowed, and Gabrielle blinked, trying to regain her composure. She marveled at the looming castle that seemed to come from a fairytale, with its towering spires and ancient stone walls.

So . . . this was Fenshire Castle.

It was even more beautiful than Gabrielle imagined. The carriage came up to a drawbridge, the horses' hooves striking the wood loudly. They passed a moat filled with lovely swans, and she half-expected trumpets to herald their entrance.

Past the archway was a conglomeration of carriages, as well as riders on horseback, as though arriving for some event.

In the melee, someone caught her eye.

Astride a tall, black horse of some sixteen hands was a strikingly handsome man with dark hair, who turned at Gabrielle's arrival.

She had craned her neck to look out the window, and locked gazes with him. He mesmerized her for several heartbeats. Then his lips pulled back into a smile, as he gestured with a gallant nod.

With her pulse quickening, Gabrielle nodded politely and leaned back into her seat.

She was here to be a companion, not a regular guest, she chided herself.

But for good measure, she allowed herself another peek at the gentleman.

Read more about Gabrielle in *Gabrielle's Gift.*

Jewel Allen is an award-winning journalist, author and ghostwriter who grew up in the Philippines and now lives in Utah. She has a bachelor's degree in English from Utah State University and runs a memoir publishing company, Treasured Stories. She writes books in several genres: contemporary romance, historical, paranormal, and nonfiction. In November 2015, she made Utah state history by being the first Filipino-American to be elected to a City Council (Grantsville). She started a four-year term in January 2016 and was re-elected in 2019. Visit her website: www.JewelAllen.com

Printed in Great Britain
by Amazon